MARKED BY THE VAMPIRE

CYNTHIA EDEN

Published by Cynthia Eden.

Cover art and design by: Pickyme/Patricia Schmitt

Proof-reading by: J. R. T. Editing

PROLOGUE

"Are you quite certain that you understand the risks?"

Olivia Maddox straightened in her chair as she met the rather doubting stare of Eric Pate, a man with enough power to basically make or break her career. Pate was a big deal at the FBI, and if she didn't convince him that she could handle this assignment, then he'd be kicking her out of that shiny office door any moment and her ass would be bouncing into the street.

Olivia cleared her throat and tried to appear like she was in control as she said, "I have a PhD in criminal psychology, and I have spent years studying and profiling some of the most infamous killers in the United States—"

He waved that away. "Fantastic for you, really," he cut through her words, sounding everything but impressed. "But when we talk about sending you into Purgatory, well, we're sure not talking about letting you mix and mingle with your run-of-the-mill *human* killers."

Her heart raced in her chest, but she schooled her expression to show no emotion. She knew that he would be looking for a sign of her fear, and she didn't want to appear weak before him.

Pate's nostrils flared a bit and his green eyes narrowed on her.

"I am aware that the prisoners at Purgatory aren't...human," Olivia said. This was rather tricky. Most humans didn't know about the werewolves and the vampires. They didn't realize that paranormals were right beside them every day and night, hiding in plain sight.

Most paranormals weren't looking to hurt or kill prey. But some...*some* very dangerous werewolves and vampires seemed to relish giving pain to humans. It was those particular individuals who found their way to Purgatory, the only paranormal prison in the U.S.

It was a prison that wasn't even supposed to exist. Modeled after Alcatraz, Purgatory sat on a small island off the coast of Washington. No prisoner there was ever supposed to escape. *Once you enter Purgatory, there is no going back.* The inmates there were vampires and werewolves who'd lost their control and attacked — *killed* — humans.

When it came to the paranormals in the area, Eric Pate was the man in charge. "I know that you're in charge of Seattle's Para Unit." An elite FBI team that was far, far off the books.

"And how do you know that?" His voice was mild, curious.

She figured it was time to put all of her cards on the table. "Paranormals attacked me once. Werewolves — they came after me. I've known for a long time about their existence." Others could pretend that monsters weren't real, but she'd never wanted to hide from that truth.

Instead, she wanted to understand the monsters. Olivia needed to know why some became such brutal killers yet others maintained their control perfectly and were able to live side-by-side with humans.

"That doesn't explain how you know about the Para Unit. It just explains how you know about the wolves." He raised one brow as he studied her. Eric Pate was a handsome, powerfully built man in his mid-thirties. He was also a guy that she definitely didn't want for an enemy.

"Senator Donald Quick is the man who referred me to your office." And Donald was an old family friend, a man who'd helped Olivia when she'd been at her most desperate. "He's the man who got your Para Unit up and running. *He's* the one who gave me clearance to learn about the work you do."

"Yes...and he's the one who insisted on this little meeting." A flash of anger appeared in Pate's eyes. "I don't like having *assignments* forced onto me."

Wait, was she an assignment?

"Senator Quick spoke highly of you, but when it comes to Purgatory, I just don't know that you have what it takes..."

Olivia's spine hurt because she was holding it so straight. "I've interviewed serial killers. I've seen the carnage they left behind, and I've seen *into* their minds." Her breath whispered out. When she inhaled again, her lungs seemed to chill. "Humans or paranormals...they can both be monsters, and it's my job to understand *why* they turn into killers."

Silence. Silence that stretched far too long. Oh, that couldn't be a good sign.

"I can handle myself," she assured him. "I am not some green rookie. I am the woman who has the best knowledge to get this particular job done."

She kept holding Pate's stare because to look away then would be a sign of weakness. Pate would pounce on any weakness, she knew it. His head cocked as he studied her, and that silence kept right on stretching.

"There are only two ways to access Purgatory," Pate finally said, "by ferry or by seaplane. The seaplane only lands for emergencies, and the ferry goes across *one* time each week."

He is going to send me there. For an instant, she almost felt light-headed.

"The werewolves are collared with silver, so that keeps them contained, and the vampires are given diluted blood—"

"You mean drugged blood?"

His lips curled into a smile that was just cruel. "Would you rather we allowed them to remain at full power? These aren't some romantic, sweet, glittering vampires. These are savages that have been placed in that hell because they've killed, again and again, without mercy."

Her palms were sweating.

"And *you* want to go in there with them?" Pate still seemed doubting.

"Not all werewolves are killers. Not all vampires go dark and drain their prey to the point of death. If we can find out *why* these individuals have lost their control, then perhaps we can help others." That had always been the point of her research. To understand the killers so that she could *save* lives.

But Pate shook his head. "Sometimes, there is no why, Dr. Maddox. Sometimes, there's just evil."

She didn't want him to be right about that, but she knew...*he is.*

"One month. I will give you access to certain inmates for one month, but I want you to forward me all of your case files and notes immediately after you complete each research session with the Purgatory inmates."

"But confidentiality —"

Pate's laughter filled the room. "You don't understand what's happening here. Things at Purgatory are not quite what they seem. There are certain individuals in power who thought it was a brilliant, damn idea to get all of the most dangerous Paras off the streets and into Purgatory."

So the humans would be safe.

"Then there are others..." His hand slid over the hard line of his jaw. "Others who think it was the worst, fucking plan ever to get so many powerful Paras in one place. When you bring that force together, what do you think can happen?"

Chaos. Hell.

"One month," he said again, voice hard, eyes glittering with intensity, "and you give me all of your research data."

The deal was going to be her only way into Purgatory. "One month," Olivia agreed as she stood. Her skirt slid down to brush against her knees as she offered her hand to Pate.

He rose slowly. His fingers curled around hers. "Get packed, doctor. That ferry will be leaving at 5 PM."

Her eyes widened. She gave a fast nod and pulled away from him. Olivia hurried toward the door. She'd have to make a mad dash to Wellswright University in order to get her notebooks and files and—

"They'll be able to smell your fear there."

His words stopped her just as Olivia's hand reached for the doorknob. She glanced back at him. "Excuse me?"

"They'll know you're human. Weak. Prey. They'll smell your fear, and they'll like it."

She gulped, and remembered the instant earlier in the interview when his nostrils had flared and his stare had hardened on her. *Is Eric Pate human?* Her gaze slid over him. He looked human, but most paranormals did...until they were ready to let their beasts out to play. He was tall and muscled, and a predatory air clung to him.

Monster...or man?

"Once you enter Purgatory, I won't be able to help you."

His words made goosebumps rise on her arms. "There will be guards there." She swallowed and hoped her voice would sound less raspy. "Surely they can protect me."

"If hell breaks loose, look for a dragon. He might be able get your ass to safety."

She had no clue what the guy was talking about. "Right. I'll just look for a dragon." As far as she knew, there weren't any dragon shifters. *Oh, please, don't let there be any!* Fire terrified her, and a giant reptile-like beast that was basically a fire-breathing snake? *No. No, thank you.*

Olivia opened the door.

"Good luck, doc..." Pate's drawling voice followed her from the room. "You're sure going to need it."

CHAPTER ONE

Olivia ran to the edge of the dock. She was late. Embarrassingly, ridiculously late for the ferry. It had taken her too long to gather all her files from the university.

Olivia's heels rapped over the wooden dock as she raced for the boat. She was clutching her briefcase—containing all of her precious files—in one hand, and her other hand was frantically waving toward the ferry. "Wait! I'm here!" Big, fat raindrops plopped down on her as she ran.

Olivia rushed forward. The ferry was still tied up to the dock. They weren't leaving her. They weren't—

"ID." A towering, bald man with tree trunk arms appeared in her path.

Olivia almost slammed into him, but she managed to stagger to a stop just in time. Then she fumbled with her coat pocket and pulled out her ID even as the rain dropped down harder and harder.

The guy scanned her ID. She noted the gun at his side. Correction—*guns*. He had a gun strapped to each hip. She had no doubt those guns were loaded with silver bullets.

"You're clear." His voice was cold, as cold as his gray eyes.

She hurried past him and hopped onto the ferry. The waves were starting to get rough, and the boat rolled beneath her. "I'm so sorry that I'm late," Olivia began, voice breathless, "I had to rush back to the university to—"

Her words ended in a dead stop because she'd just gotten a look at the other passengers on that ferry.

Three armed guards, all wearing black, all with their weapons out and pointed at the man who stood just a few feet away from Olivia. At the man who was currently watching her with a predatory stare. His green eyes seemed to glow with an unholy hunger...a dark need...as they swept over her.

"Well, well," the man said, his words low and rumbling. "This trip just got one hell of a lot more interesting."

He was shackled. The chains circled his hands and his feet, but the shackles just seemed...ridiculous on him. Useless. Power emanated from him, and the guy's strong body made a mockery of the restraints. He was big, easily six foot three or four, and his shoulders were wide, his arms rippling with power and—

"Like what you see?" he asked, lifting one blond brow. "Because I sure do."

Olivia sucked in a sharp breath then she jerked her gaze *off* that prisoner. Instead, she focused on the nearest guard. "I-I didn't realize a prisoner transport was occurring today." Her heart thudded too hard in her chest.

"I'm a special delivery," the bound man said, his voice—if possible—even deeper.

A shiver slid over her, and it wasn't caused by the cold rain.

The guard she was staring at—a man with dark brown hair and dark eyes—stepped toward her. "You don't have to worry, ma'am," he told her, his Texas drawl reassuring. "This vamp won't hurt you. He won't hurt anyone again."

Helplessly, her gaze slid back to the prisoner. *Vamp?* He smiled at her, and flashed fang. Deliberately, she was sure.

Her thudding heartbeat sped up even more.

"We're losing our light!" A sharp voice barked.

She turned to see a man in cargo pants and a dark blue shirt heading toward her. A captain's hat was slipping down his forehead. "Storm is coming," he added, giving a hard nod. "The ride across is going to be damn rough."

Olivia exhaled slowly. She'd taken a motion sickness pill a few minutes ago, but she didn't know how long it would be before the thing kicked in. The boat was already rocking beneath her feet, and judging by the way those dark clouds were swirling overhead—yes, "damn rough" would probably be an apt description of their journey.

The captain stopped and frowned at the vampire. The captain's grizzled jaw locked. "Another one of your kind?"

The vampire's faint grin never slipped.

"What'd he do?" the captain asked the guards.

It was the dark-haired guard who responded. "Left a path of blood behind him."

Fear twisted inside of Olivia. Her head turned and she found the vampire staring at her. His smile widened.

They'll smell your fear.

She'd always been able to hide her fear from the human killers that she interviewed. They never saw her fear or her revulsion. Never realized that when she left them, her knees were trembling. But this man…he would know everything.

The captain grunted. "I'm gonna need help on deck." He jerked his thumb toward the vampire. "So take that guy down below and make sure he won't be trouble."

Olivia was quite sure the vamp *would* be trouble.

"Then someone needs to come up and help me through the storm."

The guards vanished with the vamp, heading down a flight of steps. Olivia held tight to the railing and tried to make her body move with the pitching waves. The ferry chugged away from the dock, and the clouds overhead erupted with a full fury. The rain wasn't just plopping down any longer—it was pelting their vessel.

She braced her feet and kept her death-grip on that railing. The farther they went, the wilder the waves seemed to become, and the wind was soon ripping at her, tossing her hair around her face and yanking at her coat.

"Go below deck!" The captain bellowed. He was sliding behind the wheel. One of the guards was at his side.

A big wave hit the side of the ferry and Olivia almost hit the deck face-first. *Going below deck is a grand plan.* She slipped and slid her way to the stairs. Then she hurried down into the darkness that waited below. The wind was howling now, the storm a vicious monster, and she wondered why they just hadn't waited. Hadn't tried to come out on that ferry the next day. Wouldn't that have been better?

Another hard wave must have hit the ferry at that moment because the boat shuddered and Olivia fell down the last two steps. She tumbled down and —

He caught her.

She felt the cold metal of the vampire's restraints against her arms as he caught Olivia in his strong grip. He lifted her up, holding her easily against him.

"Let her go!" A guard snarled.

The vamp didn't.

The light over them was flickering. The flickering light let her glimpse the vamp's expression. His gaze seemed to see right *into* her. "Better be careful," he told her, his voice the deep rumble that Olivia knew she'd never forget. "You don't know what waits in the darkness."

Oh, she had a pretty good idea.

"Let me go," she told him softly. This vampire didn't seem drugged. Not at all. Had he started that diluted blood intake yet? He appeared far too powerful. "If you don't let me go, that guard is going to stake you." Her words were a real threat because the guard had already pulled out a wooden stake.

Instead of letting her go, the vampire pulled her even closer and he — inhaled?

"I like the way you smell," he told her, and she felt the slight movement of his mouth against her ear as he whispered, "I didn't expect to find something so sweet on my way to hell."

Her hands were braced against his chest. The ferry was shuddering from side to side.

"Shane," the guard snapped, "don't make me do this to you."

Shane.

The vampire laughed. "And don't make me kill you, Philip."

But the vamp—Shane—he slowly let her go. As soon as his hands dropped, Olivia jumped back as if she'd been burned, and she did feel that way. As if he'd burned her or marked her somehow, just with his touch.

"You okay, ma'am?" Philip asked her, that Texas drawl strong in his voice.

She nodded but didn't look away from the vampire.

"You're going to make things difficult," Shane told her. "Wonder how many dumb bastards I'll have to take out there…because of you?"

She shook her head, totally lost.

"I guess we'll see…" Shane shifted his body a bit.

Her gaze fell to his shirt-front. She'd grabbed his shirt when she fell, and she'd yanked open the top few buttons there. She could just make out his golden skin.

Her gaze swept over him, studying him now in that faint light. His right wrist was turned toward her, and, curving around that wrist, she could just make out the faint edge of a tattoo.

She inched forward, still staring at that tattoo.

The ferry dipped to the right.

That tattoo…it almost looked like…

The ferry shuddered to the left. She grabbed onto the wall for support.

It looks like a dragon's wing.

Her gaze rose. Shane was staring right at her. Smiling. Showing his long, dangerous fangs. And looking at her with a fierce desire glowing in his eyes—a desire that said the vamp would sure like to take a bite…of her.

***

The restraints were a joke. Shane August knew that he could break free of them in less than ten seconds time. It would take another ten seconds to eliminate his guard and then—well, then he could enjoy the delectable treat staring at him with such big, dark eyes.

She wasn't letting fear show on her face. Impressive. Most humans usually cracked quickly when they were afraid. But her expression didn't reflect her terror, but her scent did. Fear hung in the air around her. Fear because of the storm. Fear because of *him*.

He knew who she was, of course. Pate had briefed him on Dr. Olivia Maddox. Shane had been planning for this particular undercover assignment for weeks.

But he hadn't counted on the Hot Doc.

Pate had totally screwed him on this one.

You work to get Intel your way. Pate's words played through his mind. *And let Dr. Maddox work the inmates her way. She may be able to uncover information that you can't.*

Right…because all the monsters in Purgatory would take one look at her and start salivating. Just like he was doing.

She was all curves and smooth, golden skin. Her hair—long and black—had escaped from the twist she'd worn when she first stepped onto the boat. Now that hair slid over her shoulders, glistening with water.

Her lips were parted faintly, and he sure liked her mouth. The doc's lips were wide and full, and he wanted to feel her mouth beneath his. No, he wanted *her* beneath him, and that damn well wasn't going to work.

He had a mission. He couldn't afford to get distracted, no matter how hot the doc might be.

She is plenty fucking hot.

His tongue slid over his fangs. Oh, but it would certainly be fun to have a little bite of her.

"Stop it," Olivia snapped, some fire shooting through her voice as red stained her cheeks. "I'm not on your menu."

Are you sure about that?

Philip jerked on Shane's restraints. Ah, Philip — a transport guard who had no clue who Shane truly was. The guy just figured Shane was another inmate. He certainly had the fake rap sheet and sentencing papers to go along with that cover.

But Shane wasn't a cold-blooded killer. He'd killed, yes, but all of his recent hunts had been sanctioned by the FBI.

It had been years since he'd let the darkness inside of him loose. But once he stepped inside of Purgatory, all bets would be off.

The ferry rolled again. He heard one of the guards beside him swear. The guy was rather green looking. Humans.

"Help! I need more help up here!" The captain bellowed.

Shane just kept his body braced as the ferry rolled. He could hear the thunder of lightning outside.

Philip pulled Shane toward the cell on the right. That had been their destination just before the delectable doctor had fallen — quite literally — into Shane's grasp. Shane didn't resist the guard. What would have been the point of that? But he did take his time strolling into that cell. The door — composed of heavy, silver bars — swung shut behind him.

"Jennings, you keep an eye on him," Philip ordered.

It looked to Shane as if Jennings could barely keep his lunch down.

Philip touched Olivia's shoulder. "He's contained. You don't have to worry."

Yes, she did.

Philip hurried up the stairs. And Olivia —

Well, well…

She came closer to Shane. She was smaller than he would have liked, probably only around five foot four or five. He was much bigger and stronger than she was. If they both survived Purgatory, he'd have to be careful with her.

"You don't seem afraid." Her words were soft.

He stepped closer to the bars, the better to inhale her scent. *Delicious.* "Why should I be?"

"Because you're heading to prison."

His shoulders lifted in a shrug. He could see the pulse pounding at the base of her throat. Racing so frantically. He'd like to lick her there.

Then bite her.

"Prison doesn't scare me," Shane said. Those words were true. Nothing scared him. He'd lived too many centuries for fear. When you'd faced all the darkness that he had, there was no room for such a human emotion.

Especially when he'd never been human.

Her gaze slid over him, as if she were searching for something.

The ferry tipped again, a hard slant, and her fingers flew out and locked around the door's bars as she tried to steady herself.

Jennings slumped against the floor, covering his face. The guy even let out a moan.

The human guards were making deadly mistakes. If he'd wanted, he could have killed them all so easily.

If he'd wanted...

Shane's hands lifted. His fingers brushed overs hers. Olivia's hands were soft, warm. "You're the one who should fear Purgatory." He was trying to warn her. Pate should never have sent her in. Shane didn't care what kind of mind games the lady could play with killers. She was in way over her head.

"I'm not a prisoner." One of her dark brows lifted. The lights were flickering over them, but he would have been able to see her perfectly in the darkness. "You're the one caged."

"You...you should back away from him," Jennings managed to huff out. The guard appeared to be turning green.

She didn't back away. Foolish or brave? He decided she might be both.

"You have a tattoo on your wrist."

Now she'd just caught him by surprise. "Admiring me, were you?"

The boat rolled again. He felt her hands tighten around the bars. She shouldn't have been afraid of falling. He had her.

"It looks like a dragon's wing."

Shane didn't reply.

"Is it?"

Jennings had made it back up to his feet. "Get…get back, doctor. He's dangerous."

You have no idea.

He let her hands go. Took a step away from her.

Slowly, Olivia slid back.

He kept his eyes on her. The delectable doctor had noticed his tat—one that had been a real bitch to get since he healed from most injuries. But the artist had been used to working on vamps, and that ink had been a very special blend.

Once upon a time, he'd battled his share of dragons.

Now, he would battle different beasts in prison.

The doctor staggered a bit as she headed for the stairs. A few seconds later, she fled into the storm.

Laughter came from him. She wasn't going to escape from him…once the ferry reached the island, they'd both be trapped in Purgatory.

***

They'd made it to the dock, to Purgatory.

The rain was still falling in heavy bursts, plummeting down as Olivia made her way off the ferry. Armed men were waiting to meet her, all wearing guard uniforms.

One man advanced toward her. "Dr. Maddox?" He offered his hand to her. "I hope the crossing wasn't too difficult."

It had been a nightmare. But she'd managed to keep her cool. The poor guard, Jennings, hadn't been so lucky. He'd been viciously sick several times.

She took the man's offered hand. Felt his calluses against her fingers. As his hand held hers, she was caught by his bright, blue gaze. A very cold gaze.

"I'm Warden Case Killian." Another guard rushed up with a large umbrella, one that covered both Olivia and the warden. Case let go of her hand. "Pate told me that you were coming." He motioned to the guards and another one took her bag. "I've prepared temporary quarters for you, but you must be aware that we live a very Spartan existence here. I hope that won't be a problem for you."

"No problem at all." She tried to sound brisk and efficient, a hard task since her teeth were chattering and her clothes were soaked.

The warden gave a nod. "Good." Then he was turning and leading her toward the heavy stone walls of the building.

Purgatory resembled an old stone castle far more than it did a prison. High towers rose from each of the four corners of the facility, and she could make out the shadowy form of guards walking along the walls up above.

She hurried to keep up with Case, but Olivia found herself glancing back over her shoulder.

The vampire was being taken off the ferry.

"We only transport prisoners once a week." Case's voice drew her gaze back to him. "We have to make sure all of the others are in lockdown then." The heavy doors were opened for them at the entrance to Purgatory. When Olivia stepped inside, the silence was immediate.

Even the roar of the ocean stopped. She just heard…nothing.

This time, her shiver had nothing to do with the cold.

"We have to be very…careful about our new arrivals. Containment is always a priority," Case added.

She pushed back her hair, sending droplets of water falling around her. The place looked like something from the Middle Ages on the outside, but inside the facility, technology was everywhere. Video cameras. Computers. Sensors.

"Every cell is monitored, twenty-four hours a day. Security was increased substantially because of an...incident that occurred a while back." Case's gaze raked over her. "Thought you'd be older." He shook his head. "Hoped you'd be uglier."

Her jaw dropped. Had he seriously just said that to her?

"But it is what it is." He motioned to the guards. "Let's take the doctor to her room and get her settled."

That was it? Well, hell, what had she really expected? A red carpet welcome? "Thank you," Olivia said, her words rushing out. "But I-I was hoping to see the inmates and—"

"Tomorrow. Pate has already sent a list of the inmates you can access. Though why the hell you want to talk with them is beyond me."

Shane had entered the prison. Case's gaze shifted to him. The warden's eyes narrowed. "They're all evil, straight to the core," Case said flatly. "Prison is a waste for them. They should just be put down."

She was looking right at Shane when Case made that announcement, so Olivia saw the emotion in the vampire's eyes. A quick flash of rage that darkened his gaze.

"But then, they don't all survive Purgatory," Case continued as a faint smile curved one side of his mouth. "Here, they have a way of taking each other out."

That was barbaric. Terrifying. "I thought this place was a humane punishment—"

Case shook his head and never looked away from Shane. "They're not humans. Never forget that."

Being a Para didn't make someone a monster. Everyone deserved fair treatment.

A guard was heading toward Shane, and the guard had a syringe in his hand.

"What is that?" Olivia asked. She'd been told about diluted blood, but she hadn't been told—

"It'll make the transition easier for him. Once the prisoner wakes up, he'll be fully contained."

Drugged.

Her gaze flew to Shane's. Only he wasn't staring at Case any longer. His eyes—dark with a vampire's power—were on her.

"Don't worry about me, love," Shane assured her. "This won't hurt a bit."

Two guards grabbed his arms. Held him tight. Obviously, they expected Shane to fight.

Instead he…

Blew her a kiss?

Her eyes widened.

Then the needle was plunged into his neck.

Two seconds later, Shane hit the ground, unconscious.

***

Shane waited until his cell door shut, then he slowly cracked open his eyes. The drug was pumping through his body, but it wasn't weakening him. Very little *could* weaken him, and that was why he'd been chosen for this particular assignment.

He listened for a moment, using his enhanced hearing to monitor his surroundings. He could hear the shuffle of footsteps. The rasp of breathing.

He inhaled. Smelled blood. Decay. The ocean.

And…her.

If he could smell her, the others would too.

Slowly, Shane rose to his feet. There were bars on his window. A big, wide window, but one covered with long, silver bars. When the day came, the sunlight would pour in, and the bars would keep *him* in. Rather clever—giving the vamp the sun view. The warden wanted him weak.

And sunlight *did* weaken most vampires, just as the drug did.

Shane curled his fingers around the bars, but instead of the cold metal, he remembered touching silky smooth skin.

"Let the games begin," Shane murmured.
In the distance, werewolves howled.
He smiled.

CHAPTER TWO

"We keep the vampires separated from the werewolves," Case told her as he escorted Olivia along the stone walkway that led to the northeast tower. A new day had dawned, the storm was gone, and the sun shone brightly overhead. "If we didn't, they'd kill each other right away."

She looked down below. She could see a large group of men, all wearing prison uniforms, filling a small courtyard.

"We let the vampires out during the heat of the day. They're at their weakest when the sun is high."

Her gaze slid over the crowd. "How often do they receive blood?"

"Once every two weeks."

That wasn't very often. But she knew why the warden had set up that blood schedule. The more blood a vamp received, the more powerful he or she was.

Olivia licked her lips. "And the werewolves? When do they get out?"

"Right after dawn, but they always wear their silver collars." He paused. "Are you familiar with the collars?"

A bit.

One brow lifted. "Your friend Pate created the collars."

It wasn't as if Eric Pate was actually her friend. Was he *anyone's* friend?

"The collars are lined with tiny needles. Those needles can send silver straight into the werewolves' blood stream. You get a wolf who tries to fight us…" Case shrugged. "And you're looking at a prisoner who is about to get pumped full of enough silver to incapacitate him."

Such cold words. She knew that silver in the blood stream would be the equivalent of having fire burn from *within* the werewolf's body.

Case continued, "I assure you, security here is top notch. I took over last month, and I made *sure* Purgatory was contained."

That was an interesting choice of words. Her focus sharpened on him. "And before that? You mentioned an incident last night."

Case's handsome face hardened. "A few prisoners tried to escape before I was put in charge here. Their attempt failed, and they were killed." He shook his head. "No one escapes Purgatory."

They entered the tower. More guards waited. Guards were everywhere at that place, and video cameras monitored every single inch of the prison. Case pointed to a room on the right. "It's been used for interrogation in the past, but it'll be your interview room now."

Right. Time for her to get started. Her shoulders squared as Olivia marched inside. Her nose twitched a bit at the strong smell of bleach in that room.

"We got all the blood out for you," Case said as he propped his shoulders against the back wall and watched her. "Thought you'd prefer it that way."

She didn't flinch. "Kind of you." Just how much blood had been in the place?

His head cocked as he studied her. "Have we met before, Dr. Maddox? Because you sure seem familiar to me."

"I don't think we have." She made her way around the table. Organized her files.

"Are you quite certain?" A darker note had entered his voice.

"We haven't." She would have remembered him.

"Um…" The guy didn't sound convinced. Too bad for him. The warden wasn't exactly making a stellar impression on her. There was something about him that unnerved her. And after spending so much time with killers, her nerves were usually much stronger.

Footsteps approached her little room. She knew those steps belonged to the guards. No doubt they were bringing in her first research inmate. She'd been given the list of interview subjects right after she'd gone to her temporary quarters, and unless she was very wrong about one of the names on that list—

"Hello, again, love."

He's here.

Shane stood in the doorway. He was smiling, flashing his fangs.

Shane Morgan. She'd read through his file. Actually, she'd read it four times. Maybe five. Shane Morgan was a vampire who'd been found guilty of killing four men in a Chicago bar. According to the notes she'd reviewed, he'd never shown any remorse for his crime.

And the prosecutor had strongly suspected that Shane had killed many, many other times before he'd been caught that dark and deadly Chicago night.

"I was hoping to see you again," he said as his stare seemed to stroke right over her. There was definitely a sensual edge to those words.

Olivia's hands flattened on the table. Sunlight streamed into the room, *onto* Shane, but he didn't appear at all affected. "I'm here to ask you some questions."

The guards pushed him into the room. Shoved him into the chair across from her, and locked manacles around his wrists. The manacles were attached to the heavy stone in the floor.

"Love, you can ask me any damn thing you want."

Case stiffened and shot away from the wall. "Watch it, vampire."

"Ah…Warden Killian, isn't it? What a fucking unpleasure it is to meet you."

Case's expression darkened. "Vamp, you need to —"

"Warden, I need you to leave the room while I talk with the subject," Olivia said quickly. The last thing she wanted right then was a confrontation between those two. *No more blood on the floor!* Now she was realizing why the place had been bleached.

She didn't want a brawl right in front of her. And if Shane felt threatened, hell, he definitely wouldn't open up to her. She *had* to get him to talk. Olivia cleared her throat and told Case, "I've found that I can get individuals to talk more freely when —"

"You want me to leave you alone with a vampire?" Case stared at her as if Olivia were totally insane.

I'm not. "The sun's up. He's chained. He's no threat."

Shane laughed softly.

"And the cameras are on." She didn't like them, but there they were, watching and recording their every move. "If anything happens, I'm sure a guard could be in here in less than a minute." Because she knew there were guards watching those video feeds.

Case's hands had fisted. "You could be dead in less than a minute's time. *Before* the guards had a chance to get in this room."

That was not an ending she was particularly planning for right then. "I've been alone with killers before. I assure you, I can handle this."

A muscle flexed in Case's jaw, but after a moment, he gave a rough nod. "Have it your way." But he didn't head for the door. Instead, he stalked toward Shane and stopped when he was less than a foot away from the vampire. He glared at the vamp. "Move to hurt her in any way, and I'll throw your ass in solitary."

"Is that supposed to scare me?" Shane asked, voice curious.

Case moved closer to Shane. "You haven't seen my solitary confinement...yet." The threat hung in the air.

Olivia realized that she was barely breathing.

Then Case pulled back. He nodded once more to her and headed for the door. The guards filed out after him. When the door swung shut, the clang seemed to echo around her.

"Take a breath now," Shane advised her.

Her breath rushed out.

Shane's lips tightened. "You shouldn't be in this damn place."

She sat down in her chair. The wooden chair legs wobbled beneath her, much like her own legs had a tendency to do. "I'm only here temporarily," Olivia told him quietly, "but unless I'm wrong, I think you're here for the next hundred years." Give or take a decade.

He leaned toward her. The chains stretched a bit with his movement. "We'll see about that."

She looked into his eyes. They were strangely beautiful eyes, compelling and deep. Flecks of gold were hidden in those green depths. He was handsome, dangerously so, and she wondered if he'd used his good looks to lure in prey over the years.

"I do wish I could read your thoughts," he murmured as he gave a slow shake of his head.

"I'm here to find out why you kill," Olivia blurted, then her lips clamped shut in horror. She'd meant to be more tactful. Meant to lead up to that part, but, well, her nerves must have taken over and those words had tumbled out.

"Are you now?" His fingers drummed on the edge of the table. "Then let me save you some time. I kill because I'm a vampire. That's sort of our thing."

Lie. "Not all vampires kill their prey. Not all vampires even drink from live sources. Some drink from blood bags and never even touch live prey at all." How did some survive so easily that way? While others seemed to love the violence and fury of murdering a human?

His green gaze held hers. "Lions don't let their prey just wander away after they take a little bite."

No, lions didn't. Their powerful teeth tore into their prey. They devoured.

"Half of the thrill is in the hunt…the other half is in the victory of the kill." Shane pushed back his shoulders. Seemed to focus totally and completely on her.

Just as she was focused entirely on him. Olivia wouldn't make notes on their meeting. Not yet. She'd wait until he'd left her, then she'd gather her thoughts about the vampire. "You were hunted once." She had to point that out. "That's how you became a vampire." She wanted to see if he could have empathy for his victims. Because, once, he'd been a victim, too.

But his expression didn't change.

"Do you remember being afraid?" Olivia asked him.

"I've never been afraid."

"Sure you were. Everyone is afraid of something." She found herself leaning toward him. Mirroring his movements was part of her strategy. Trust building. Her subjects always talked more when they felt secure with her.

"Is that so?" His chains creaked again. "Then why don't you tell me what you fear…Olivia."

How had he known her first name?

"I heard the guards talking about you," he murmured. "When a sexy young doctor walks into hell, people take notice."

It wasn't hell. It was Purgatory. And her muscles were too tight. "This interview isn't about me. If you're not going to participate in the session, I can call the warden back in here. There are plenty of other vampires I can have brought in. I don't have to talk with you." Pate had picked him, not her. She could find someone who unsettled her a bit less.

"Ah...*so there's an answer*. You fear me." He nodded, as if he'd just had a theory confirmed. "I thought as much." He gave what looked like a rather sad shake of his head. "You probably shouldn't have gotten yourself locked in a room with a man you fear. Not such a smart move, love."

"Stop calling me love." This was professional. An interview. Nothing more.

Nothing less.

"*Love*, I truly fear nothing because I have already lived through every hell imaginable."

She believed him. The truth was in his eyes and his voice.

"Tit for tat, is that how this will be?" Shane asked. "You reveal to me...and I reveal to you?"

The last thing she intended to do was reveal her own secrets. "That's not how it works. I'm not the prisoner here."

"Aren't you?"

She stared down at his files. "You killed four men in Chicago. Why?"

"Why not?"

Her right hand fisted. "There are other vampires..." She was already going to be interviewing three more. "I don't have time to waste with you."

Silence. She knew he was waiting for her to look up at him. So she didn't. She kept staring at those files as if they truly fascinated her. As if —

"You shouldn't mourn those men. They weren't some innocent humans. They were killers, too."

Her gaze lifted.

He'd leaned toward her even more, stretching out those chains that bound him. "Is that what you want to hear, *love*? That they were evil, and I only kill *evil* humans? Will that make the crime better for you?" His words were low, deep, wrapping around her.

Olivia shook her head. "No. I want to hear the truth."

He smiled then. "No, you don't. No one ever does."

She was getting nowhere with him. Normally, she could take months to build up trust so that her subjects would talk to her. Pate hadn't given her months. Her clock was ticking down every moment.

"What is it like when you kill?"

The chains squeaked. "You're more blood thirsty than I realized."

You have no idea.

Olivia had to keep pushing him. "Do you ever think about your victims or is the attack just about…you?"

The color of his eyes darkened. *Vampire.* "It's always about me, love, *always.*"

***

Case turned away from the video screens. Dr. Maddox hadn't recognized him, and that was damn good. He'd pushed her deliberately, to see if she might remember him, but she hadn't. He'd only been in her presence once, briefly, years ago. Obviously, he hadn't made a big impression on the woman.

But then, Dr. Maddox had always been more interested in the paranormals than the humans around her.

That was why she was there. Her interest in monsters was the reason that they were *both* there. He started to pace. The interview was still going on, but the vamp wasn't telling Dr. Maddox anything new. As far as Case was concerned, there was only one reason why the paranormals attacked. They killed because that was the nature of their beasts. You didn't need a fistful of degrees to figure that shit out.

He whirled back toward the screen. Dr. Maddox and the vampire were leaning toward one another. The vampire looked as if he just couldn't wait to take a bite out of the lady. Shane was still bound though, still chained securely and—

Case saw the end of the chain begin to rip away from the floor.

Fuck!

***

When she heard the groan and pop of that chain, Olivia surged to her feet.

But it was too late. He'd ripped the first chain from the floor. The second followed an instant later.

Her breath heaved out as she waited for the vamp to go right for her throat.

Only he didn't move.

"I told you…" Anger hardened his voice. "You'd be dead in less than a minute." His eyes burned with fury. "So the next time you get a prisoner in here, make damn sure you have a guard with you."

The door flew open behind him. Case rushed in, with two guards right on his heels.

Shane leapt to his feet and whirled toward them.

"No, don't!" Olivia cried out, but the guards had already fired their weapons. The bullets slammed into Shane's chest and he stumbled back against the table.

She grabbed for him, clutching his shoulder. His head turned and his eyes met hers.

"Why did you do that?" Olivia whispered. He'd known the others were watching. Had he *wanted* to get punished?

"Solitary!" Case shouted. "Throw his ass in the sun for twenty-four hours, and let's see how he likes it!"

Shane's eyes began to sag closed. She realized he'd been hit with tranq darts. "Remember…always…guard…"

He was trying to protect her? The cold-blooded killer wanted her to have a guard at her beck and call? *What. The. Hell?*

Case's hands wrapped around Olivia's shoulders and he pulled her away from Shane.

Then the vamp was dragged out of the room. His chains trailed behind him.

***

Sunlight. Burning from every wall. Burning down from the ceiling. From the floor.

"Neat little cell, isn't it?" Case asked him as he shoved Shane into solitary. "Scientists can invent the most amazing things. I mean, it's not real sunlight, but your kind gets weak from ultraviolent radiation, too, right? I mean, this is like one big ass tanning bed." He laughed. "So I'm sure you can see just how much fun this place will be for you."

The light blazed all around him. For an instant, Shane remembered another time. Another place.

He'd been tied to the ground. Wooden stakes had been driven into his hands. His chest. *But the fools missed my heart.* He'd been pinned there, helpless, as the sun rose.

The sunlight hadn't killed him then.

It wouldn't now. *If the real sun can't kill me, this fake shit won't take me out, either.*

But being tossed into solitary on his first day in Purgatory…that *would* help him. Playing by the rules in that place wouldn't get him the contacts he needed. He had to prove himself as an alpha vampire, he had to be willing to take the pain that would come…and Shane had to be ready to destroy anyone who got in his way.

He tilted back his head and let the light sweep over him.

He knew the drill. After all, he'd done his research on this place. On the new warden. The guy liked to play with the prisoners. After he thought Shane had been weakened enough, the warden would toss Shane into the yard so the other vamps could have a go at him.

That's when they'll see I'm not their prey.

A new alpha vamp was in town, and he'd learn all the secrets that Purgatory possessed.

***

"I kill because I like it." The werewolf in front of her pushed a hand through his midnight black hair. "I enjoy watching the light drain from my prey's eyes. In that last moment, the victim knows that I have all of the power. Life or death, it's all on *me*."

Revulsion twisted Olivia's stomach, but she kept her gaze on the prisoner before her. In the last twenty-four hours, she'd heard stories to give her enough nightmares to last for the rest of her life.

As if she didn't already have enough of those.

She'd talked to two other vampires. Begun the process of getting them to open up with her. But the thing about vampires…they didn't just have a few years of bad deeds behind them. The powerful vamps—the vamps in Purgatory—had *centuries* of horror to share. And they had…almost gleefully.

But the werewolves were different. Or at least, the other two that she'd interviewed had been. They talked about their attacks and their beasts as if they were separate entities, as if they had no control over what happened when they were in wolf form. Regret had tinged their voices.

But not this one.

David Vincent slouched in his chair. He'd spread out his legs and arms to take up as much space as he possibly could. The silver collar gleamed around his neck, a silver the exact shade of his glittering eyes. He was a man in his prime, probably around his mid-thirties, with the powerful build sported by most of his kind.

"You don't feel that your...beast...made you kill?" Olivia asked him carefully. The sun was shining through the big, open window. Bright and hot. She could just hear the murmur of voices outside of her window. The vampires were in the courtyard below.

"The beast and I are the damn same. I do what I want."

Alpha.

She nodded slowly. She'd suspected he might be an alpha werewolf as soon as she started reading his files. His attacks had been particularly brutal, and, since coming to the prison, he'd made a point of attacking other werewolves.

Those who challenged his power?

"You have no regrets about what you did?" The others had expressed remorse. There had been loathing in their eyes. Not a hate directed at her. At themselves.

"It's survival of the fuckin' fittest. I'm the fittest." He leaned forward. "I always survive."

No matter what he had to do.

"You were infected with a werewolf bite five years ago." Those details had been in his file. Most humans didn't survive a werewolf bite. But certain individuals had DNA that let them...transform. A genetic coding was there for some individuals so that when they were bitten, they didn't die. They became beasts.

Werewolves.

Before his bite, David Vincent had been a boxer — a man who'd enjoyed the battles that came his way. A bump lined his nose, silent testimony to his old bouts, and faint scars crossed his knuckles. "What happened to the werewolf that bit you?" Olivia asked, curious about that.

"I baked him a fucking thank you cake," David growled at her as his lips twisted in a savage smile. "What the hell do you *think* happened to him?"

Well, fine. If he wanted to stop the little dance, then so would she. "I think you killed him as soon as the change was complete for you. You hunted him down, and you made him pay for what he'd done to you."

That twisted smile slipped a bit from his lips.

"Darkness grew in you after that kill. Because you liked it. You liked the way it felt to take a life. So you hunted and you killed again and again. You kept killing, kept feeling that thrill, until you were locked up…" She glanced around at the stone room. "Here."

His chair scraped as he pushed back. Her hand slipped beneath the table. She had the remote for his collar right there, and her fingers slid over it. If he made one move toward her, she was supposed to send a surge of silver at him. Through him. But she suspected the guard standing less than five feet away would beat her to that punch.

He had a remote for David's silver collar, too.

"If you know so much about me," David snapped, "then why bother with your lame ass questions?"

"Because I know your crimes. I want to know *you*." Her breath heaved out. "Did you try to fight the cravings? When the urge to kill came, did you try to stop? Did you spare anyone?" *Was there ever any hope?* Or, once the darkness came, was it too late?

David glanced away from her. His gaze locked on the window. Her body tensed. *Avoidance.* "David?"

"You can try to fight the dark, but when instincts take over, control doesn't last real long."

"So you did try to stop." Now excitement quickened her blood. "You can *still* stop. You can fight what you've become. You can—"

His head jerked toward her. "I will kill anyone who gets between me and what I want." Said with absolute certainty. "And I will have a fucking blast while I do it."

Chill bumps rose on her arms.

The voices rose outside of her window. Shouts filled the air.

Her gaze jumped toward the streaming sunlight.

"Just like they're having a fucking blast now…" David murmured. "Vamp blood is gonna stain that yard."

The guard moved so that he could better stare out that window. Whatever he saw below made his body tense.

"Wh-what's happening?" Olivia asked as her heart beat faster.

"My guess is…that new vamp is about to lose his head. That happens here, more than you would think." David's words had her focusing on him. That savage smile was back in place. "Survival of the fittest…"

The new vamp—that was Shane. It had to be him! Olivia jumped to her feet and ran toward the window.

Sure enough, she saw Shane standing in the middle of the courtyard. The other vampires had formed a circle around him, but no one was touching him, no one was attacking him, not yet. They all stood back, maybe a foot or two, as they shouted their insults and threats at him.

"Get the guards down there," Olivia ordered. She'd brought the silver remote with her, and her sweat-slick hand held it easily.

The guard near her—Brett McKey—lifted his radio. "Courtyard. Got a 666 occurring."

"What's a 666?" She'd never heard that code on any police scanner before.

David laughed. "It's a monster beatdown. But don't worry, I'm sure the guards will all get down there in time for a nice, up-close view of the bloodbath."

She didn't see any guards closing in. She only saw—

The crowd attacked. A pack of big, powerful vampires lunged at Shane. They covered him completely as they took him down.

"No!" Olivia screamed. "The sun is up! They're supposed to be weak!"

There was a faint rustle of sound behind her. "Funny thing about that..." David's voice rasped. "Things here aren't always how they're *supposed* to be."

"Sit back down, wolf," Brett snapped. "Sit the hell back down, *now*."

Olivia didn't glance back at the men. Her gaze was on the battle below. She could hear the snarls and the growls and a splash of blood already stained the ground. "Stop!" Olivia yelled. "*Stop!*"

Then the first vampire flew back into the crowd. It was one of the men who'd attacked Shane. He was just—just thrown through the air like a rag doll.

A second vamp followed him.

So did a third...a man with blood gushing down his chest.

The crowd stopped screaming then.

She could see Shane once more. His left hand had locked around the neck of one of his attackers. His right hand had curled around the throat of another. He was holding the other vamps easily. Seeming to exert no effort at all. As she watched, stunned, Shane tossed one of the vamps straight into a stone wall. The last of his attackers squirmed in Shane's hold, kicking and punching, and Shane just...he laughed.

"I'll be damned," David whispered.

Olivia jumped at that whisper. David was right beside her. She hadn't heard him close that distance at all. She'd been too focused on Shane and the fight below.

She whirled toward the werewolf. Too late, Olivia saw Brett on the floor behind him, his body twisted. Oh, hell, *no*.

"Boo," David said, and then he grabbed for her remote.

She hit the button on it even as his fingers locked around her wrist. The collar was supposed to send silver straight into his bloodstream as tiny needles shot from the collar and into his neck. He should have fallen back then. Should have stopped.

He didn't.

He grabbed the remote from her. Smashed it in his fist.

Then he yanked her toward him. "Now…*I get to ask the questions…*"

***

The crowd was silent around him. Hell, yes, they were backing up. They should back up.

Was that vamp pack attack supposed to have been scary? Was that supposed to have been a challenge for him? Even after twenty-four hours in solitary, kicking their asses had been too easy.

He rolled back his shoulders and waited to see which fool would come at him next. Shane even started to smile —

A scream ripped through the silence.

His head jerked up. His eyes locked on the window in the west tower. The room *she'd* used to interview him, and he knew that scream was Olivia's. He *knew* it.

The scream cut off abruptly.

Hell, *no*.

More vampires swarmed toward him. They must have thought it was time for round two.

He stared up at that window…

And felt hands grab hold of him.

***

David had yanked Olivia with him and toward the door. She thought he was going to try and escape, but instead, he shoved the table and a filing cabinet in front of the door, sealing them inside.

"That'll buy us some privacy," David said.

No, this *wasn't* happening.

The silver collar *should* have worked. It hadn't.

The guards who'd been monitoring the video feed *should* have been rushing to her rescue.

Were they coming? *Hurry!*

His grip was so tight on her wrist that Olivia feared he'd shatter the bones any moment.

"What are you?" David demanded as he yanked her closer and then he—he *smelled* her. Sniffed her.

Her free hand shoved against his chest, but he didn't let her go. His mouth hovered over her throat and he seemed to be drinking in her scent.

At least he's not ripping my throat out, not yet. "I'm a psychologist. I'm here to try and profile—"

"*What are you?*"

Olivia's gaze flew frantically around the room. Brett was on the floor, his eyes closed. He was breathing, but that was about all she could say for him in that instant. "I-I'm a human..."

"Liar." He said the word as if it were a caress. "I wonder...are you what I've been waiting for?"

She screamed again. Loud and long even as she kicked at him. Punched.

He just smiled.

He likes the fight. He told me...he likes it.

Olivia stilled.

His smile slipped.

"I'm human," she said, struggling to keep her voice calm. Panic and fear had overwhelmed her for a moment, but she had to stay in control. Help would come. She just had to stay alive long enough for it to arrive.

"Let's see about that…" And, before she could even draw another breath, his fingers — his claws — cut into her wrist.

Don't let him bite me. Don't.

Blood slid down her wrist. Dropped to the floor.

"I bet the vamps down there can smell your blood," he said. "Wonder if you smell like a human to them?"

The vamps were still shouting. She was staring into David's eyes and seeing his beast.

Where are the guards?

He let her go. Just…let her go.

Olivia stumbled back. She sank down to her knees, as if she were too terrified to stand.

"Let's have a taste…" David lifted his hand. His fingers were covered with her blood.

Her fingers slid inside her boot.

He — he licked up a drop of her blood from his claw. Closed his eyes. Seemed to savor her taste. *"What. Are. You?"*

Olivia leapt up, the small silver knife held tightly in her hand. Olivia always, *always,* kept that knife hidden in her boot. The guards at Purgatory had never searched her, so they hadn't known about her weapon. She drove that knife right toward David.

Just before the blade would have sunk into his chest, David's eyes flew open. He grabbed for her hand, and the blade missed his heart. It sank into his side, and he roared his fury and pain. His claws came at her —

"Don't fucking try it." A low, lethal voice. One that was coming from…the window?

David froze. Then his head turned toward the window.

Olivia was already gazing at the vamp there with wild shock, and desperate hope.

Shane. Shane was in the window. She didn't even know how the hell he'd gotten up there. *Had he scaled the stone wall?* But she was just so glad to see him that —

He's a killer, too! He's not a hero here to help you.

Her hope crashed as the voice of reality screamed in her head.

"Smelled the blood, did you, vamp?" David taunted. "Don't worry, I'm sure there will be plenty to go around."

Shane jumped down. His feet hit the stone floor and he started stalking toward David. "Come to me, Olivia."

Her blood trickled down her inner wrist.

"If you do, he'll make a meal of you," David promised her. "The vamp will gulp you all down. The last thing you'll ever feel on this earth will be his teeth tearing into you."

Yeah, well, she'd already felt the werewolf's claws slicing into her. Unlike the werewolf, Shane hadn't hurt her. Yet. She inched toward him.

David grabbed her. "*My* prize, vamp."

Shane's gaze dropped to Olivia. "He hurt you."

"The collar isn't working." That was obvious. She hated the tremble of her voice.

"It's all right," Shane told her softly. "He won't hurt you again."

David's rough laughter rang out. "I've got plans you don't even—"

Shane lunged across the room. Moved so fast she barely saw him. One instant, David was holding her tightly, his claws far too close to her throat, and in the next moment, she was behind Shane as he faced off against the werewolf.

"She's not *yours*," Shane snarled. "So don't ever touch her again."

The two men stood with their bodies tense, muscles locked in a battle-ready post. Both tall, strong, powerful in different ways.

But…the sun was up. David should've been stronger right then.

She crept toward Brett. Her hands slid over the downed guard. There was blood matting his hair, and the remote that he'd had was still secured at his waist. Fumbling, she pulled out that remote.

"You trying to claim her?" David demanded, his voice rising. "You think you know what she is? I tasted her, I tasted the power, and it's going to be *mine!*"

Her head whipped back toward him. His claws were out and he was—transforming. Right then, right there, starting to shift into the deadly form of a wolf. *This shouldn't happen! Not when he's wearing a collar!* But his jaw was elongating, his bones snapping and—

She pressed the buttons on Brett's remote. Frantically, she pushed every single button.

David screamed, an unholy cry of pain as he fell to the floor. His claws scraped over the stone even as his body arched in agony.

She hit the buttons again.

He slammed, face-first, into the stone, as his body went limp.

Shane whirled toward her. His breath heaved out and his hands were clenched into fists.

His fangs were showing.

And she didn't have a stake handy. The sound of her ragged breathing filled the air.

He stepped toward her.

"Stop!" Olivia ordered. Right. Because that was supposed to do some kind of good. Her order to him. Shane kept coming toward her and then he—

Offered her his hand?

"Love, I told you this place was too dangerous."

She blinked at him.

He pulled her to her feet. Held her injured wrist in his hand.

"Do *not* bite me," she told him, and her voice only shook a little. Okay, a lot.

"Tempting..." His fingers held her carefully. His gaze was on the wound.

Footsteps thundered outside of the door. "Dr. Maddox!" A desperate shout.

She recognized Case's voice. The cavalry had come.

"Your rescue party is a bit late." Shane's jaw locked. "That werewolf could have killed you long before that idiot and his men got inside."

"How did you get inside? I mean, how did you get up to the window?"

His head lowered toward her. "It's not the first time I've scaled a tower."

She shook her head. That feat should have been impossible, even for a vamp. To get up that wall, so fast...

"I have to do this," he told her then, just confusing her more. "I'm sorry, but I have to know why..." He started to raise her wrist to his mouth.

"No!" Olivia shouted as she tried to pull against him. He was even stronger than David. "Don't!"

His eyes glinted at her. "He didn't kill you."

The guards were shoving at the door. She could hear their desperate efforts to get past the makeshift barricade that David had put in place.

"He tasted you...a werewolf's senses are the most acute of any paranormal." His eyes raked over her. "What the fuck has Pate done now?"

Her jaw nearly hit the floor. "P-Pate?"

He put his mouth on his wrist.

"Don't!"

His lips pressed to her skin and he...he licked her. Tasted the drops of her blood there. And while his tongue slid against her skin, his eyes held hers.

The guards broke through the door.

"Get away from her!" Case yelled. "Now!" But he and the others were already running toward Shane.

"Interesting," Shane murmured. "Very, very interesting..." He kissed her wrist. Then he let her go. He swung to face the armed guards. "It's about time you all joined the party."

She could practically feel the fear filling that room. The guards must have witnessed Shane's display of power in the courtyard, and now they were afraid of him. Olivia knew they were right to fear him.

"Get the vamp in a cell! Get that damn werewolf out of here!" Case barked orders. His gaze landed on Brett. "And get a medic!"

Shane didn't fight against the hands that grabbed for him. He did look back at Olivia, though. His gaze held hers. "Love, I like the way you taste."

She put her bleeding wrist behind her back. Lifted her chin. "That's the only taste you'll ever be getting." She could still feel his mouth against her flesh. Like a brand. Hot. No, scorching.

His laughter drifted back to her as the guards led him from the room.

Other guards dragged David out of there even as two of the medics rushed inside. Olivia backed up, trying to make room for them. She backed right into Case because he'd closed in on her.

"The vampire bit you?" His eyes were narrowed with fury.

"No." She shook her head. Glanced toward the window. The courtyard must have been at least forty feet below them. "He saved me."

"Bullshit."

Brett let out a low groan.

"It's true. David—David is the one who attacked me." *What are you?* His words seemed to echo in her head. "He attacked Brett and…" Her breath rushed out. "My remote didn't work on him."

Case's eyelids flickered.

"Why didn't the guards come in immediately?" Brett was being carried out on a stretcher. "They were watching. Why didn't they come in as soon as he attacked?"

"Because your vampire hero was causing a near riot downstairs. All hands were needed. You had a guard in here," he gritted out as fury darkened his gaze. "We thought you were *safe*."

And she'd thought her remote would work. "What happened to the remote? Why didn't it work?"

His gaze slid over the floor. He bent then and picked up the shattered remains of her remote. "Because it's smashed to hell and back? It's hard to work when it's in pieces."

He was a jerk. "David smashed it *after* – "

A medic tapped her shoulder. "Miss, do you need stitching up?"

Her wrist was still throbbing. She could still feel Shane's mouth on her skin. "Yes." The medic carefully pulled her toward the door.

"Where did the knife come from?" Case asked quietly.

She looked down and saw the bloody, silver knife near her feet. "I had to protect myself." When the damn remote stopped working.

"You smuggled a silver knife into my prison?"

"I had to protect myself," she said again. The medic was still pulling her toward the door.

"Why didn't they kill you?"

At that question from Case, Olivia tensed. But she had an answer. The only answer that made sense. "Because David likes to play with his prey. He wasn't done playing with me."

"What about Shane?"

She glanced back at him. "You got here in time." *Lie.* There was so much more to Shane than she'd realized. The vampire wasn't at all what he appeared to be.

That was fine. She wasn't exactly what she appeared to be, either.

***

The cell door slammed shut behind Shane. They hadn't thrown him back in solitary. Probably because they realized solitary wasn't doing a damn thing to him.

He closed his eyes as he stood in the middle of that cell. He could still taste Olivia on his tongue. A taste that was far too sweet, like candy. A taste that had sent a surge of power flooding right through him.

He knew the taste of humans. He'd sampled too many of them over the years not to know their taste.

Olivia looked human. She smelled human. She sounded human.

But she tasted...like something different. Like something special. *Something I need to have.*

Olivia wasn't human.

He knew it, and now...so would the werewolf.

***

David slowly opened his eyes. The collar on his neck burned because the damn thing was still pumping silver into him.

They'd caged him again. Put him in the solitary confinement area designed just for werewolves—a small, two by five box with silver walls.

He laughed as he sat in his hell.

The guards had no clue. No fucking clue.

The instrument he'd needed had just been delivered right into his hands. Finally, *finally,* he could start his attack.

And the humans could die.

CHAPTER THREE

Olivia opened the door to her temporary quarters—and found a guard standing on the other side. Her heart jumped in surprise because she sure hadn't been expecting the guy. "I, um, didn't realize I'd have an escort this morning." The night had been hell. Every time she closed her eyes, she'd seen not David—not his claws.

She'd seen Shane. He'd been in her mind all night long.

He mentioned Pate…Shane knows that Pate sent me in to Purgatory.

"I'm not your escort, doctor. I'm here to make sure you stay in the room you were assigned to."

Wait, what? Olivia shook her head. "I'm not a prisoner here."

He just stared back at her.

"The federal government sent me in here!" The freaking FBI! "I'm supposed to be interviewing the inmates!" She hurried forward.

He blocked her path. "I'm sorry ma'am, but Warden Killian sent *me* here. You aren't to get past me. You're to stay in your quarters until the ferry comes back on Friday."

That was *days* away. "You are kidding me."

"He said your assignment at Purgatory is over." Sympathy flashed on his face, but his tone didn't soften. "So until the boat can come back for you, I'm afraid you don't get to leave this area."

The hell that would happen. Fury pounded through her body. "Get your warden on the radio. *Now*. I have connections that man can't even dream about." Such a giant lie. She had one connection, but she would sure use it. "How does he think I got here in the first place? And if I do not get to continue my job, Warden Killian and you are both going to find your asses facing questions from the FBI."

The guard swallowed and his Adam's apple bobbed nervously. He hesitated a moment longer.

"Get that radio!"

He snatched up his radio.

Olivia's wound throbbed. *Something is wrong here. Very, very wrong at Purgatory.* Every instinct she had was screaming at her, and Olivia only knew one thing with certainty.

She had to see Shane, immediately.

"I wish you'd get out of my way," she snarled at the guard. "Just — *move.*"

His face went slack with shock, and, surprisingly, he did.

She took that opportunity, and Olivia ran past the guard as fast as she could. *I won't be locked up like the prisoners.*

Because she wasn't one of them.

***

Shane's head whipped up. His heart drummed even faster in his chest. He could hear the sound of frantic footsteps coming his way. He inhaled, catching the scents around him —

Just as the footsteps turned and started running in the opposite direction.

"Olivia." Her name escaped from him as a growl. He grabbed for the cell door, and he yanked the thing right off its hinges.

The vamps in the cells around him began to yell.

"Get me out, man!"

"Break my fucking door!"

"He's out, he's out!"

He ran past them, following the sounds of those fleeing footsteps. The steps weren't heading toward the vamp wing any longer. They were rushing toward the part of the facility that housed the werewolves.

He sped faster after her — and it *was* Olivia he was pursuing. He'd taken her blood, and now…hell, now he could track her any place. Any time.

She'd never escape him.

He rounded the corner and saw her just before she could disappear into a long corridor.

Shane snagged her wrist, and his fingers slid over the white bandage that covered her wound. She spun around, her hands tight, little fists, and one of those fists drove straight into his jaw.

Work on that hook, doc. Work on it.

"It's me," he whispered. Video cameras had to be watching, and he had pretty much screwed his cover to hell and back, but maybe he could still make this work…maybe…if he played things just right.

He pinned her against the nearest wall. Caged her with his body.

"What are you doing?" Olivia demanded, her voice high and sharp.

His body pressed to hers. Desire surged through him when he felt her curves against him. And when she twisted, rubbing her soft body against him…a groan broke from Shane's lips.

"I need your help!" Olivia said. "I need — "

He kissed her. For two reasons. Reason one…because he had to stop her from talking before the woman shredded his cover by saying the wrong thing.

Reason two…he fucking wanted her mouth.

Her lips were open, and he liked that — oh, but it made things easier. His tongue slipped over the edge of her lips, slipped right inside her mouth, and she gasped.

His body pressed ever closer to hers. Her hands were against the wall, held captive by his grip, and her mouth—she was kissing him *back*.

The desire he felt surged ever stronger within him. Her mouth opened more for him, and her soft lips moved lightly against his own.

He would have fucking kissed her forever…if he wasn't sure they were about to be in some serious danger. So, hating it, Shane pulled his mouth from hers. But then he kissed her jaw. Her stubborn and damn adorable jaw, and then, with his mouth close to the shell of her ear, he whispered, "Surveillance—audio and video. Watch what you say."

He could hear the thunder of her heartbeat.

"Dragon…" He barely breathed that word, but he knew she needed the reassurance it would give her. He'd tried to clue her in yesterday, but, this time, he needed her to fully know that she could count on him.

Her body trembled against his. "I knew…last night…"

He licked her ear. Just for the hell of it. The ear was there, he liked the delicate shell, so he licked it—and she trembled again.

His cock stiffened even more. And her pulse was so close. Racing. If he just bent down and kissed her neck that frantic pulse beat would be beneath his mouth.

"Something is wrong here…my…my silver remote didn't work yesterday. And it took the guards too long…to help me."

He pulled back, just a bit, to study her. In the distance, he could hear the sound of metal doors clanging. Security was coming. But they'd been too slow about it. The guards must have seen them on the video camera, and they'd just *left* Olivia alone in the hallway with a monster.

"I think they wanted me vulnerable. And—and Case is trying to keep me locked up." Fear flashed in her eyes. "This wasn't supposed to happen. I don't understand—"

"Why the hell do you keep going after her?"

Shane had known the warden was leading the march toward him. Instead of answering the warden, he leaned down and pressed a hard, hot kiss to Olivia's lips.

The guards grabbed him and hauled Shane back. He broke free of them, and squared off against the warden. "Why? Because I fucking like the way she tastes." And he *still* hadn't recognized her taste. He'd never encountered it before.

She's half human. Has to be. She smells like a human.

What was her other half?

Case's eyes blazed with fury. "Tranq him until he can't move."

"No!" Olivia cried out as she leapt in front of Shane. "Don't do that, he's —"

Shane caught her shoulders and yanked her around to face him. He made sure his fangs were out as he drove his head toward her throat.

The tranqs hit him. Thuds in his back. His sides. He lost count of how many hit him.

He could feel the drug coursing through his blood.

"Don't...tell..." he managed to whisper. He hadn't been going to bite her. Not there. Not with her fear in the air around them. When he bit her, she'd ask for his bite. Beg for it. His attack had been faked so that he could get close enough to whisper to her.

His knees hit the floor, and his hands locked around her hips as he stared up at Olivia's face.

Don't tell.

She gave an almost imperceptible nod.

And more fucking tranqs hit him.

"Drain him," he heard Case order as Shane's eyelids sagged closed. "Let's see how strong he is once most of his blood is gone..."

Idiot. Shane would still be strong. Just as strong and *damn hungry.*

***

"Sooner or later, the Paras here learn that we're stronger than they are." Case's voice was smooth. Calm.

But he was pacing around his narrow office, and his pacing was sure the sign of a nervous man.

Olivia watched him from her seat. "You drain vampires… regularly?" That was torture to her mind.

He whirled toward her. "What the hell else do you want me to do? I use sunlight on them when I can, and that keeps most of them weak, but then we get the alphas in here. Alphas like your friend, Shane, and when they're ripping the freaking doors off the cells, we have to use any means that we can in order to control them." His breath heaved out. "So don't sit there and judge what we do. My men do the best they can, in a situation that no man should ever be facing."

Her stomach knotted. "You think this prison is failing."

He gave a bitter laugh. "I *know* its failing. Hell, I was sent down here to clean up the mess that the last warden made, but there's no cleaning up some things." Case had stopped pacing. His grim stare leveled at her. "This place was a mistake. They're too powerful to be kept here. Most of the time, I feel like *we're* the prisoners, not them."

"If they shouldn't be locked up," Olivia began carefully, "then they should be —"

"Dead. It's the only way to keep humans safe."

She leapt to her feet. "That's not true. We can learn *why* they've killed. Why they've hunted —"

"It's because they don't have souls! They're monsters!" He shook his head in disgust. "After what happened to you, hell, lady, you should know that."

She tried to calm her racing heartbeat. "Harold Bath."

"Who the hell is that?"

"A banker from Maine."

"What?"

"One day, Harold came home from work. He shot his wife. His neighbor. Went on a rampage and hurt ten people before the cops arrested him." She could see Harold in her mind. His slightly balding hair, his stooped shoulders. His flat voice as he said he'd just gotten tired of hearing his wife talk. "Most people would say he was a monster, but he was just a human. Twisted, but human."

Case stepped toward her.

"Lindsey Jones." Another image flashed before her. A pretty red-head with wide-set, blue eyes. "Female serial killers are rare, but Lindsey killed five men last summer along the Florida coast line and she was—"

"Let me guess," he interrupted, voice tight, "human."

Olivia nodded. "Monsters are everywhere. We have to learn *why* they kill, why they break, if we truly want to protect the innocents out there." He had no idea how personal this was for her. *Why? Why?* That single question had haunted Olivia for most of her life. What made some people crack—what pushed them over the line and turned them into killers?

And will I be like that one day?

She slammed the door shut on that thought immediately. The way she always did.

"Maybe they're just psychotic, did you think of that, *doctor?*"

"Sometimes, they are." But the cases were often about more than just a chemical imbalance or some brain defect. They were about so much more. "My job is to find out why. I'm here because I want to save lives."

"Even if you lose your own in the process?"

"I don't want to die." She'd never had a death wish.

His laughter was rough, a bit cruel. "Do you even realize how close you came to death yesterday?"

"It's not the first time a test subject has tried to hurt me."

Shock widened his eyes.

"I know the risks of my job. I can handle them." She kept her voice calm with an extreme effort of will.

"You have an alpha vampire who wants nothing more than to sink his teeth into your neck and a werewolf who nearly killed you." Case put his hands on his hips. "You actually think you can 'handle' them? Because I sure as shit don't believe you can. I don't believe—"

A shrill alarm cut through his words.

"No," Case whispered. He whirled for the door. "*No!*"

The alarm grew even louder.

"What's happening?" Olivia asked as fear pumped through her.

He yanked open the door. A guard stood there. "Sir, the prisoners—"

"Someone's trying to escape from the facility. We need to get this place locked down, *now*," Case snapped back to the younger man. He jerked his thumb over his shoulder. "Get her back to her quarters. Go via the south side of the facility—"

The guard's blue eyes widened. "That's where the werewolves are."

"I damn well know where they are." Case grabbed a weapon from the cabinet near the door. "Right now, we need to keep her away from a certain vampire, so that's the safest course. Get her back to her quarters, *now*."

The alarm was still shrieking.

Then Case was gone.

***

She could hear the growls. The corridor was dark, too dark, and it felt as if she were walking right into a cave. The growls echoed all around her. The alarm had finally stopped, and maybe that should have made Olivia feel better. It didn't.

"Why did you want to talk to the monsters?" The guard asked, glancing back at her. Evan. He'd told her that his name was Evan Jurant.

"It's my job."

He grunted, then turned back around. He pulled out a keycard and unlocked a door with thick, steel bars. He opened that door, swinging it so that it opened back toward them. He raised his hand, indicating she should go through first, but she hesitated.

Evan frowned. "Doctor?"

"This route will take me to my quarters?"

"Of course." He eased back, making even more room for her to go first.

She pushed back her shoulders and advanced. *I need to find Shane.* She'd taken about four steps when she heard the door shut behind her. The sound was overly loud. Strangely final.

"You'll have plenty of time to talk with the monsters now."

Olivia spun around. Evan hadn't followed her—he'd closed that door and he was locking it again. "No!" Olivia grabbed for the bars, but it was too late.

Evan looked as if he were barely twenty years old, but his brown eyes were so cold as they stared at her. "You're not gonna get out, doctor. They're gonna want to keep you."

The growls had died away. Goosebumps rose on her arms. She could almost…almost feel others closing in on her, but Olivia was afraid to look over her shoulder. "Why are you doing this?"

"Because I was paid, very well, for you." He took a few more steps away from the bars. "You're in the maximum security area, Dr. Maddox. Locked in with the most dangerous werewolves. I hope you enjoy your talks with them."

Then he turned. Started walking away.

"No!" She screamed after him as Olivia jerked on the bars. "You can't do this! The cameras—"

"Have all been turned off." He paused. Glanced back at her. The corridor was so dark around him that she could barely see his face. "An escape is in progress. The Paras have sabotaged some of our equipment, and by the time all of our machines are back online, well…it won't matter for you."

Footsteps rustled behind her.

"Don't do this," Olivia whispered. "Please."

His voice was hard as Evan said, "It's survival of the fittest here…sorry."

Survival of the fittest.

Behind, those footsteps drew closer. And even before she turned to face those stalking her, Olivia knew who would be leading the pack.

"Hello, again, Dr. Maddox…"

David's voice wrapped around her as a hand curled around her shoulder. She looked down and saw his claws.

Then she did the only thing she could. Olivia screamed, *"Dragon!"*

Because Pate had told her…*If hell breaks loose, look for a dragon. He might be able get your ass to safety.*

Hell had broken loose. And if help didn't come, her ass would be dead.

*** *** ***

Shane's eyelids flew open. He was on a table — an operating room table, and some bastard in green scrubs was holding a bloody knife above him.

"He's awake!" The words were a desperate gasp from behind the bastard's facemask. "Dose him again, dose him — "

Shane grabbed the knife. Broke the fool's wrist. Took the weapon and hurled it at the other idiot who was trying to come toward him with a tranq.

The knife sank into the man's arm and he fell, screaming.

Humans…always so weak.

Just as I'm…weak…

Shane glanced down and saw the blood that soaked him. There were long slashes on his chest. His arms. Fury pumped through him. "*What. The. Fuck?*"

"I-I was just following orders," his soon-to-be-snack stuttered. "Just—"

Shane sank his teeth into the man's throat. Blood poured onto his tongue and some much needed power pulsed within Shane.

"*Dragon!*"

The cry reached him, so very faint, and he yanked his mouth away from his prey. Olivia?

He strained, but heard no more screams.

His prey whimpered within Shane's grasp. "Give me weapons," Shane growled at him. "Give me your access codes…"

The man stared at him, his eyes widening as the fellow seemed to go slack within Shane's grasp.

I have his blood. I can control him. He'd been controlling humans for centuries. "*Give me everything I need,*" Shane commanded.

His prey nodded.

***

David laughed. "Dragons? You won't find them here, pet, just wolves and bloodsuckers."

Olivia could see at least six other men behind him, all crowding in on her. All wearing collars that should have controlled them, but their claws were out and their teeth had lengthened and seriously sharpened.

"I thought they were putting you in solitary," Olivia whispered to David.

He smiled at her, and the sight made her stomach knot. "You also thought they were keeping you safe." He leaned toward her. David trailed a claw down her cheek. "Are you tired of being wrong yet?"

She nodded. "I really am."

He laughed. The claw scratched her skin, and blood dripped down her cheek. Her back was pressed to the bars, shoved hard against the door as if she could find escape that way.

She couldn't.

And she couldn't get through the pack of werewolves in front of her.

"Most of the guards are on the north end of the prison. They think vamps are trying to escape." David shook his head. "But there's no need to escape, not when the thing we need is right..." His claw slid down her throat. Paused over her frantically racing pulse point. "Here."

What he was saying made no sense to her. Why would he possibly need her?

"I'll find out how to use you," David promised her, "even if I have to slice you open to find out your secrets."

This couldn't be happening.

"You're mine, djinn. *Mine.*"

What the hell had he just called her? She pushed harder against those bars, wishing with all of her might that the door would open and—

The door opened. She fell back, heading right for the floor, but strong arms caught her before she slammed down. Those arms lifted her up—and against a powerful body.

"*Got you,*" Shane whispered.

Then the werewolves attacked.

CHAPTER FOUR

Shane shoved Olivia behind him even as he jumped forward and rammed the door back into place. He pushed hard, using his enhanced strength, because those dick werewolves were trying to keep that door open.

But the silver bars were burning them. The silver didn't burn him. With a ferocious roar, Shane slammed that door back into place.

David's claws flew out at him, fitting between the bars as the werewolf tried to go for Shane's throat. "You're dead!" David shouted.

Shane backed up, just one step, so that his jugular wouldn't get sliced by those swinging claws. "*Un*dead is the correct term, jackass. Get it right." He bared his fangs at the wolves. "Guess who gets to stay in a cage?"

"*Give her to me!*" David's fury had darkened his face and made his eyes flash.

"Sorry, but I think I'm keeping her." *And why the hell did the werewolf want her so badly?*

Olivia grabbed Shane's arm. "We have to get out of here. The guard—Evan—*brought* me to them. Just locked me inside with them and left me."

Sonofabitch. He needed to get her off the island. If the guards were selling her out, there would be no safe place for her there.

I warned Pate. Did he listen to me? Hell, no.

Pate never listened to anyone.

His fingers locked with Olivia's. David began to laugh then.

"You know," David said, "you know…and you think you can control her? *I saw her first.*"

He didn't know anything right then—well, anything except the fact that he and Olivia were screwed. "The fuck you saw her first." He pulled Olivia back down the corridor. He had all of the infirmary doctor's keycards and access codes. He'd find a place to hide Olivia, then he'd make sure he got her off that island.

Somehow.

"I want her magic!" David bellowed. "I'll have it—even if I have to claw through you to get her, vampire!"

Those claws weren't hurting anyone right then. Shane's hold tightened on Olivia. What kind of magic did the woman have? This whole situation was one serious screw-up after another.

He took off running with her then because he didn't know how long he'd have before the guards closed in or before the werewolves got out.

Pate had thought that he'd taken out all of the corrupt staff members at Purgatory. Talk about thinking *wrong.*

But at least Shane knew the layout of the place. He'd studied maps of the prison for days before he'd gone in undercover. He'd looked for places to hide. Ways to escape.

Because he'd been aware that the mission could go to shit at any moment.

Guess what? That moment happened. He swiped the keycard at another turn, rushed through the door that opened, then he went left, nearly flying down a flight of stairs and—

He yanked Olivia closer. Pinned her to the wall, and put his hand over her mouth. "Not a sound," he ordered because he could hear the others…coming toward them.

Two guards, running fast, both armed with tranqs. He could kill them, quickly and efficiently, but Pate had ordered him to keep the human body count down as much as possible.

But if Olivia alerted those guards, the option of life for those two would be out of his hands.

Olivia had frozen against him. They were in the dark shadows underneath the stairs. To her, he was probably just a big, heavy shadow, but he could see her completely. Her eyes were wide as she stared up at him. Her hair was a wild tumble around her shoulders and —

Her lips had just moved against his palm. His cock stiffened because he was pretty damn sure he felt the lick of her tongue.

He yanked his hand away from her mouth.

Her breath rushed out. "Are we —" Olivia began, her voice the faintest whisper.

But he covered her mouth with his because he wanted that tongue of hers against his. He kissed her deep and hard, and he loved the feel of her body crushed against his. Lust rose within him. Physical lust because he'd wanted her from the first moment he saw her. Bloodlust because the fool doctors had taken too much of his blood and he hadn't taken enough from them.

He remembered the taste of her blood, such a delicious sample he'd had. Her blood had given him a rush of power unlike anything he'd felt before.

He needed more of that power.

He also needed her, naked and moaning, beneath him.

But not there. Not then. Shane forced his head to lift. "The guards are gone." Time for him and Olivia to haul ass. He still had her right hand in his grasp, and he started pulling her again, leading her down into the underbelly of the prison. If they were going to get out, then first they'd have to go down…and straight into the dark.

Behind him, her breath came in quick pants as she tried to keep up with him. Slowing down wasn't an option, so when he hit another flight of stairs, he just picked her up and slung her over his shoulder.

"Shane!"

He ignored her struggles and moved as fast as he could. The warden and the others would realize he was gone soon. The alarm from earlier would prove true. Someone *was* about to escape from Purgatory.

Me.

He hit the bottom floor, and saw the grate to the right. A grate that was supposed to be reinforced with silver to keep the werewolves from ever trying this particular escape route... provided that the wolves even realized it existed.

No one else is supposed to know about it.

Carefully, he put Olivia back on her feet.

"I'm not a sack of potatoes!" she snapped at him.

Really? Shit, like he didn't know that. "You're welcome for the ride and the rescue." He curled his fingers in that grate and heaved. The grate popped free—hell, yes! "Get in," he ordered her.

She crouched, peered inside. "There are going to be...things in there."

Things? His teeth snapped together. "And there are werewolves upstairs who want to tear you apart."

She shot through that opening. He followed her, moving gingerly as he tried to put the grate back in place. He couldn't get it in as securely as it had been before, but he mostly managed to wedge it back up. Someone would have to look very closely to be able to see that he'd moved the thing.

He turned around and bumped right into Olivia. "I-I can't see anything," she whispered.

Because the tunnel they were in was pitch black. The place was old, centuries old, a tunnel that could crumble around them if they weren't careful.

"Hold onto me," he told her softly. "I've got this." He could see everything, including the *things* that she'd worried about.

Her fingers clamped around his arm. "Are we just going to hide out down here? They will find us, sooner or later, or we'll just—"

"I've got a plan, love. Trust me." He advanced into the darkness.

Her nails sank into his skin. "*No.* Look, dammit, I get that it's too little, too late, but I wasn't exactly high on choices upstairs."

He frowned down at her. She wasn't looking at his face in that total darkness, but instead staring just over his shoulder.

"Give me something here, other than *dragon* – I mean, make me know that I'm with the good guy."

Oh, but he couldn't do that. He'd never been exactly good, not even when he'd been working with the FBI. If she only knew the things he'd done, she might just run back up to the wolves. "I work with Pate."

"Give me *more*. Why are you at Purgatory? What's going on?"

He pulled her closer. Wanted to take her mouth again but didn't. *Control.* "We don't have time for a fucking long discourse here, love. So here are the simple facts. I'm working undercover – a cover that I blew for you. And right now, I'm the only thing standing between you and death, so if you want to die, then by all means..." He let her go. "Don't trust me."

In the darkness, he saw her wrap her arms around her stomach. "You...you haven't killed? Your file was all lies?"

"I've killed plenty." Brutal truth. "And that's why I'm your best hope of survival."

She rocked back on her heels. "Have you killed innocents?"

The woman was so naive. "There are no innocents in this world."

Her body trembled. He could see the small ripple that shook her.

With his back teeth clenched, he demanded, "Now are you coming with me or do you want to try your luck with the wolves?"

Her hand lifted, tried to find him in the dark. He stepped toward her so that she touched his chest. "He called me a djinn."

I heard him. "Are you?"

"Am I what?"

Fuck. "A djinn?" If she was, then they were in for a whole world of trouble.

"No! I don't—I don't think so." Then, softer, "Is that like a genie?"

He caught a scent drifting toward him. Familiar. Human. *The warden.*

Hell, hell, *hell.* "Come on. *Now.*" And they were off, moving through the tunnel at a breakneck speed, and the tunnel narrowed as they fled. Going down, down, and the scent turned heavy with mold and earth as the darkness swelled even more, ever deeper.

She didn't speak again, and Olivia moved quickly, not asking about...*things*...even though he saw them scurry across their feet.

Then he could smell the salty air. The ocean. And hear the lap of the water.

"Please tell me a boat is waiting up there." Her voice held a desperate edge.

He whirled back toward her. The water bubbled up about ten feet away. If they dove *into* that water, they could swim out and get to the other side of the island. A place of safety, for the moment. "Tell *me,*" he told her, "that you're a good swimmer."

Silence. Then she shook her head.

He had the worst fucking luck. "Then, love, you'd better hold tight to me." She was trying to back away. Very much *not* holding tight. So he picked her up, but he didn't toss her over his shoulder again. Instead, he cradled her in his arms. "When you need to breathe, kiss me."

"Wh-what?"

"And I'll give you my air."

He ran toward the water, and, with her in his arms, leapt in.

***

Case Killian stormed into the quarters he'd given Olivia Maddox. He grabbed her bag, rifled through it. Found nothing but clothing—and a wooden stake.

"Where the hell is she?"

He'd already made Evan talk. The idiot had been blubbering when Case left him in the infirmary…with those two doctors who were bleeding messes, courtesy of the vampire Shane.

Evan had said that Olivia would be with the werewolves—only she hadn't been. The doctor had seemingly vanished.

Shane has Olivia. It was the only thing that made sense. The only reason why Case couldn't find them. The vampire was unlike any other that Case had seen. Too powerful. Too dangerous.

He spun around to face the guards in the doorway. "Search every inch of this facility. Find the missing vampire and find Dr. Maddox." His gaze fell to their weapons. "Forget the tranq. If you see Shane, kill him." Because the vampire wouldn't destroy Purgatory.

Case wouldn't let him.

"And bring Dr. Maddox to me."

***

Her lungs were burning. Olivia couldn't see anything in front of her but a murky darkness, and the salt water stung her eyes as she tried desperately to make out *something*.

Shane had her right hand in his grip. She was trying to swim with her left hand and kick with her feet, but the current was pulling at her, trying to rip her away from Shane.

She needed to *breathe*.

He'd told her to kiss him when she needed air, so she turned frantically in the water, trying to get closer to him, trying to find his—

Shane pulled her against him. His other hand came up under her chin, and his mouth pressed to hers. Her lips parted, and he breathed for her. Into her. A quick burst and then he had his arms wrapped around her. He was shooting them up, up out of that darkness.

Her head broke through the water. Her mouth pulled from his and she gulped in and out desperately as she bobbed in the water.

The moon shone down on them. A million stars glittered overhead.

And the vampire held her easily against him.

"Thank you," Olivia whispered because she knew he'd saved her life. She didn't know what would happen next, but for that moment, they were alive. And relatively safe *in the ocean.*

The island that housed Purgatory was close, and Shane was already stroking them back toward it even as the waves heaved against them.

"Stop," she said, as she tried to pull him back. "They'll be waiting for us."

"No, they think we're still inside Purgatory right now and that buys us time."

She wrapped her arms around his shoulders. Her legs brushed against his beneath the water. "Time for what? Unless you've got a plane hidden in your pocket..." Wouldn't that be awesome?

"Time to get to a safe place."

A safe place? On that little island?

"I told you before, you have to trust me."

He'd also told her that he was a killer, but it didn't seem like she had much choice, not unless she wanted to swim back to the mainland. And drown along the way.

So she did her best to stay with him—okay, he pulled her along, a lot, as they made their way not directly to the main shore, but to the left-hand side of the island.

"We're going under again," he warned her.

"Why?" The little beach was right there.

"Because that's the only way to access the cave."

Wait, what?

"Breathe, Olivia."

She did.

They went under. She kicked and stroked as best as she could and blindly followed Shane's lead. There was no choice for her anymore.

Then, too many moments later, they were breaking through the surface of the water once more. She couldn't see anything when she came up for air, and the darkness felt suffocating.

"We'll be safe here," Shane said as he began to pull her toward—what, a shore? Inside the cave?

Her left hand flew out and landed on a rocky outcropping.

"Be careful," he warned her, then he was lifting her up, sitting her on a hard, flat circle. Water poured down her body as she crouched there, and shivers rocked through her.

He came up beside her, she heard the rush of water falling off him, but even though she strained, Olivia couldn't see him. The darkness there was too complete.

"We'll be safe here," he said, and the words sounded like a promise.

She pushed back her sodden hair. Her teeth were starting to chatter. "Where is…here?"

"An old cave. There was an entrance to this cave on the island once, but it collapsed years ago." His body brushed against hers, and she jumped because she hadn't realized that he'd sat right next to her. "Now the only way in is through the water."

Her breath heaved in and out in too fast pants.

"There are some cracks along the cave's ceiling, and they let air in. Maybe even some light that will hit us later. We'll be fine here."

"Until?" There had to be an *until*.

"Until we can make a run for either the seaplane or the ferry."

The shivers hit her even harder. "The ferry won't be back for a few more days."

"The seaplane will be here in sixteen hours."

Her panting stopped. *Sixteen hours?*

"It's scheduled for a medical supply run then. We just have to get on that seaplane and fly off this island."

Oh, was that all? "They'll be watching." They...the guards. The werewolves?

"Then we have to make sure they don't stop us." Said with grim certainty. "But first..." Then his hands were on her, pulling her toward him, pulling her shirt *off*.

"Wait! Stop!" Olivia shouted at the handsy-vamp. He'd saved her ass, yes, but that didn't mean—

"You're about to shake apart. The cold doesn't do a thing to me, but it can hurt you. It can *kill* you." His fingers brushed against her bare abdomen. "Now get naked and let me help you."

Okay, right, so this wasn't about sex. The kiss under that stairwell had thrown her, and when he'd started to strip her, she'd assumed...Olivia cleared her throat. "You, um, can you turn around or something?"

"No." He yanked her shirt up. Tossed it. Reached for the snap of her pants.

Olivia realized she'd lost her shoes some place in the ocean. She also slapped at his hands because he was not just going to yank her pants off.

"*Olivia...*" Her name was a growl. "I can help you."

Another shiver rocked through her and she was pretty sure her teeth rattled.

"Vampires don't feel cold like humans do." He caught her hand, brought it up to his chest. His skin was warm, so wonderfully warm beneath her hand. "I can make it better for you. Let me help you," he said once more.

She undid the snap of her pants. That warmth was too tempting, and she was *freezing*. She pushed the pants down but kept on her panties and her bra. Clothing rustled near her and she heard the slap of his wet garments hitting the rocks.

He came back to her a few seconds later. "Move back a bit. It's flat behind you."

She scooted back.

"And, love, you need to lose the sexy bra and scrap of panties."

Olivia pretty much hated that he could see everything in the dark. "They stay on."

His hands wrapped around hers and then — then she was tumbling down on top of him. Because he was lying on the flat, rough space, and she was now sprawled all over the vamp. He wrapped his arms around her even as her legs slid between his powerful thighs. He held her tightly but…carefully…and the heat of his body slowly sank into her.

Her mouth was against the curve of his shoulder, so close to the base of his neck. After their dive, he should have smelled of salt and the ocean, and he *did*, but, more than that, he had a rich, almost heady scent that seemed to seep into her.

He was warm and solid, and he surrounded her in that darkness. Silence swept over them as they were cocooned there, and slowly, so slowly, the tremors stopped sweeping over her.

But as the tremors subsided, she didn't scramble off him. Olivia just kept taking in that delicious warmth as some of the terror she felt finally began to ebb. "Why do people think," she murmured and her lips brushed over his neck as she spoke, "that vampires are cold?"

"Because the movies say we're dead. The dead are cold. The dead don't have hearts that beat."

She could feel his heart racing.

"They say we have no passion."

She could feel, um, something *else* pressing against her. She'd been aware of his heavy arousal from the moment he'd pulled her on top of him. There was really no missing it, especially since the vampire seemed to be very well endowed.

Though she did try to shift away from him a bit then.

He just pulled her right back against him. "But our hearts beat. We breathe. We live. We need."

Need. The word seemed to echo around them.

"There's something that I need right now," he continued, his voice growing deeper, rougher, in the darkness. "Something I have to take."

She pushed up but his hands were tight around her waist. "Shane?"

"Vampires are fast healers, so you can't see where they cut me, and the blood was all washed away during our swim."

Oh, no. *No.*

"I'm hungry," those words were a deep, dark growl. "So fucking hungry…and I need *you.*"

In that instant, she was glad for the darkness because Olivia didn't want to see his face—or his fangs. "Shane, *no.*"

"I need blood." Deep, rumbling. "They took too much from me. If I'm going to protect us then *I need you.*"

Her heart was about to fly right out of her chest. "I'm scared." Hushed. "I've never…never been bitten before."

"I won't hurt you."

She wanted to believe that, but she didn't.

"There can be pleasure in the bite."

In her mind, she could only see the pictures from her files at Purgatory. The dead victims. "What if you can't stop?"

"I've been a vampire longer than you can imagine."

What?

"I can stop." Certainty thickened his voice even more. "I will stop." Then his right hand left her hip. Those fingers slid up her side, slowly, carefully, up and up…they slid around her bra and had her sucking in a sharp breath, but Shane didn't touch her breast. That hand of his kept rising until his fingers curved around her throat. Her pulse raced beneath his touch. "I just need a little, just enough to boost my strength back up."

He'd saved her, so didn't she owe this to him? She'd just feel much better about all of this if she had a stake in her hand. *Then I could make him stop.*

"Maybe you'll like it…"

She licked her lips.

"Maybe you'll ask for my bite again."

Olivia shook her head. There was no way she could imagine that. Wanting him to sink his fangs into her? No, thank you. "J-just a sip, all right? Then you'll stop?"

"I need more than a sip." There was such darkness in his words. "Need *you.*"

Her eyes squeezed shut—why, she didn't know. She already couldn't see anything. "Do it."

He pulled her back down toward him, positioned her, held her easily. She felt his breath blow over her neck, and Olivia jerked in reaction.

"Easy," he whispered. "I told you…you might like my bite."

No way. That just wouldn't *happen.*

His teeth sank into her neck. Olivia gasped at the white-hot flash of pain, it rocked through her and she was ready to fight him, to yank back because—

Pleasure lashed her. A wild, hot tide that made her whole body tense and yearn. Her hips rocked forward against the long, hard ridge of his cock as his mouth sucked along her neck. He was taking her blood, licking her skin, and she should have been repulsed.

But the pleasure wouldn't stop. It was electric, consuming, scorching her from the inside out. Incredibly, she felt her sex quaking—clenching—and a release hit her. An orgasm that had her choking back a scream because the pleasure had just ripped right through her.

From his bite?

"I can feel it..." Shane pressed a hot kiss to her neck. "Your pleasure...I can *taste* it."

His teeth pierced her once more.

The pleasure built again, coiling inside of her, twisting and stretching and she couldn't get close enough to him. Her hands grabbed his arms. Her nails sank into his skin. Her legs slid, parted, and she was over him, rubbing her sex against his cock as a wild hunger, a fierce lust that she'd never felt before, pushed through her.

In that instant, she wanted him. More than life. More than breath. More than anything.

"*Shane.*" His name was a demand. Her fear was gone. The pleasure was—

Another climax hit her and she raked her nails down his arm.

"In-fucking-credible," Shane growled the words against her. "Never...before...never..." He yanked at her panties. The fabric tore. She couldn't suck in a deep breath because the aftershocks of pleasure were hitting her.

He was naked. So hot and powerful, and his cock pushed right between her thighs.

"Take me," he told her, the words a fierce order in the dark. "I want *in*. I want *all of you*."

And the pleasure wasn't stopping. She was out of control, all reason lost, and she was the one to push that big cock into her body, to arch her hips down against him and take him inside her.

Then Olivia was truly lost.

Her sex closed greedily around him, even as he stretched her with his length, pushing her to the edge of pain and pleasure. Her body still quivered from her release and her sex seemed hyper sensitive to him.

Her knees pushed into the hard surface beneath them as she tried to balance herself. She wanted the pleasure again, wanted that hot, wild burst—

Shane heaved up, and his cock slammed deep into her. Olivia gasped out his name. His fingers clamped around her hips, and he started lifting her, up and down, fast and fiercely, again and again.

He was out of control, driving fast, and she loved it. Her head tipped back and she moaned as her body took in that frantic rhythm.

His hand slid around her hip. His thumb pushed against her clit.

"You came...*from my bite...*"

Her eyes flew open. She wanted to see him. Couldn't in the dark.

"Come again for me. Always, for me."

She wanted the release to hit. Her body yearned for that pleasure, addicted now, and she was fighting for the climax because it had been so good. Better than anything before—

His thumb pushed against her once more.

"Bite me," Olivia heard herself whisper. And she was the one to bend back toward him. To put her throat to his mouth.

There was a part of her that was horrified by what she was doing. Offering herself to him. Fucking him so wildly. But that part was small...and quiet.

The lust was dominating. She had no control then.

He bit her.

She erupted. The pleasure was even better this time because his cock was in her and her sex contracted around him. The orgasm was so strong that she couldn't even scream, couldn't do anything but shudder in that maelstrom of passion.

Then she felt him inside of her, a long, hot tide of release that just sent after-shocks bursting through her.

He pressed a kiss to her neck. Licked her skin.

She collapsed on him. Her heartbeat was drumming, a thunder that blocked out everything else. Her sex was still contracting around him, and the pleasure had her gasping because it just wouldn't stop.

Nothing had ever been like that before.

Olivia knew she should have been terrified of the way she was acting. It was too out of control. Too wild. *What I always feared.*

But with the pleasure around her, with her vampire *in* her, there was no room for fear.

That would come later. When reason returned.

***

"The vampire took Dr. Maddox." Case Killian marched in front of the guards he'd assembled. "They are somewhere on this island, and we will find them."

"Sir…"

He whirled to face the guard and saw one of the newer recruits, a blond with golden eyes, staring at him with worry etched on his face. "What?"

"How do you know Dr. Maddox is even still alive?"

"We don't know that." She'd already been gone for over two hours. Anything could happen in that amount of time. "But until we have her body, we assume that she's still breathing."

"Will he turn her?" Another question from another guard.

"I don't know what the fuck he'll do." His breath heaved out. "I just know we have to find them." And he knew exactly how to do that. The vampire had fled with the woman, but they hadn't just vanished. They would have left a trail behind. A scent.

There were no tracking dogs on the island, but he had something far better than just a dog.

He had werewolves.

The alphas are the best at tracking.

He knew one alpha in particular that would love to get his hands on Shane. "Bring me David Vincent. *Now.*" Because it was time to end this hunt.

No one escapes from Purgatory. Not on my watch.

CHAPTER FIVE

The best orgasm of Shane's very long life left him nearly gutted on that cave floor. His hands were locked around Olivia, and he was holding her as tightly as he could.

Because I don't want her to get away.

The woman had come from his bite. His fucking bite. Not just once. Twice.

Then she'd come a third time when he'd been sunk balls deep inside of her.

Sure, humans had been known to find pleasure in the bite. It could be an aphrodisiac for many, but he'd never had a woman react like Olivia had.

Her sex was still squeezing him.

And he was getting harder for her.

He should probably try to play the gentleman and pull out of her now. The heat of the moment had passed.

Had it?

He rocked his hips against her.

And felt the sudden tension that coursed through Olivia's delicate body, a body that he hadn't been able to savor, not yet. He wanted to kiss her, to lick every single inch of her.

I shouldn't have taken her here. Should have been in a big bed with fucking rose petals or some damn thing like that spread around her.

But after one taste…when her pleasure had rocked through him, there had been no going back.

Olivia's hands pushed against his chest. She rose up above him, and as she lifted her upper body, her sex pressed down harder against him, around him.

His cock thickened even more within her. One good thing about vamps, stamina was definitely their strong suit.

He caught her hands. Threaded his fingers with hers.

And in the darkness there, he could have sworn that her eyes started to glow.

A djinn.

He couldn't think about that, about the deadly ramifications if the werewolf's claim turned out to be true.

She was pushing her hips down against him again, her sex was a hot, wet dream around him, and Shane let go of his control. He wanted the wild rush of pleasure again. He wanted…her. Everything that she had to give. Every fucking thing.

And even as he drove into her, thrusting as deep and hard as he could go, Shane realized the danger he was in.

Because if the stories he'd heard over the years were true, the whispers, the legends…

He could be losing his soul right then, becoming addicted to the sensual power of a djinn.

***

"There," David snarled as he stopped and pointed to the old silver grate in the bowels of the prison. "They went in there."

Case glared at the silver grate. *How the hell did the vampire find this place?*

"Looks like someone had an escape plan," David muttered as his gaze slanted toward Case. "I didn't realize this little spot was here."

Case shoved the guy against the silver. David howled when the right side of his face hit that grate and burned. "And you'd better forget it, understand?" Yet even as he said the words, he knew it wouldn't happen. David would tell the others about this discovery. He'd use it, try to escape himself later.

And that's why I might have to kill the guy when this little hunt is over.

David was useful, and he was also expandable.

The scent of burnt flesh filled the air. Case let the werewolf go, and David jerked back. The glare the werewolf sent Case was full of fury and the promise of retribution.

Like that was supposed to scare him. "Move the grate," Case directed his guards.

It took four of them to get that heavy grate down, but, it would have been easy for the vamp to move it. With his enhanced strength, the guy had probably just given a little tug and the grate would have popped free.

"Go in," Case snapped at the werewolf as soon as the opening was clear. *"Find them."* Because they had to still be on the island. The ferry wouldn't arrive for days, and the seaplane hadn't flown in yet. *Wherever you're hiding, I will find you.*

No one had ever escaped from a tracking alpha before.

David led the way into that tunnel. Case followed, and he made sure to keep a tight grip on the remote that controlled David's silver collar. The collar gleamed in the darkness.

As they followed that long, twisting tunnel, the guards used flashlights to illuminate their path. The sound of water grew stronger and —

"I can't track them anymore." David had stilled near the edge of the dark water. Murky. Deep. A pool that would lead back to the ocean. David stared down at the water. "The scent ends here."

No, that wasn't possible. "They can't swim back to the mainland!"

David's laughter was bitter. "Maybe the sexy doctor was a mermaid in disguise. Never seen one of those before. Thought they were just myths—"

Case sent a powerful charge of silver coursing through the werewolf's collar. "They are myths!"

David sank to his knees, but his head tilted back and his eyes blazed up at Case. "That's what...people used to say...about vamps. About...werewolves..."

Case's mind raced as he considered possibilities. *Mainland, my ass.* "They just swam out and around to the side of the island. That's the only option they had. They're still *here*." He was sure of it. "We need to get outside of Purgatory's walls and search the island." He lifted the remote, but didn't send another surge of silver out, not yet. "You *will* find them."

Pain darkened the werewolf's face. The guards' lights were trained on the werewolf, so Case could see David easily as the guy rasped, "I'll find her..."

"If you don't..." Case leaned toward him. Made sure that his voice was too low for the guards to hear him. "I'll pump you full of so much silver that you'll beg for death."

He waited for the werewolf to show fear.

But, instead, the werewolf smiled. "I don't beg."

***

Olivia's eyelids flew open and awareness came back to her with a shocking rush.

She'd been asleep, curled up on the hard rocks, and she whirled around now to see —

Faint light, drifting in through the cracks and crevices in the cave. Her heart was thundering in her chest — her *naked* chest.

Because she was totally nude and her horrified gasp seemed way too loud to her own ears.

Her gaze whipped to the left and to the right. She saw her clothes, spread out, drying? And she also realized that the vampire was gone.

He'd left her. No, no, he couldn't have. Olivia jumped to her feet. "Shane?" Her voice echoed back to her. "Shane, where are you?" The pool of water was near her feet, glistening. The rocky walls of the cave surrounded her. Was there a tunnel hidden somewhere in those walls? An opening that she couldn't see in that dim light?

Olivia snatched up her clothes and dressed as quickly as she could. The clothing was still damp and it rubbed roughly over her too-sensitive skin. Skin that was sensitive because of…him.

What did I do? Why?

She'd lost herself with Shane. Her control — the careful control that she'd maintained for years — had vanished the moment he'd taken her blood.

It shouldn't have happened. It couldn't happen again.

No worries on that score, especially seeing as how he fucked me and left me.

Vampires. They weren't exactly known to be trustworthy.

Her bare feet slid over the rough flooring of the cave. She started inching toward the darkness of the walls. Her hands lifted as she tried to search for an opening, search for *some* kind of way out other than a dive into that water once more.

What did I do? Why? Why?

She could hardly remember anything about the sex with Shane — except that she'd needed him, desperately. Fire had ignited within her when his teeth sank into her neck, and she'd been overwhelmed by a sensual hunger for him. So consumed that she would have done *anything* to have him plunge into her.

He did something to me. That was the only explanation. Vampires could control their prey after they took blood from humans, and he must have been controlling her.

"Bastard," she whispered. She'd thought he was a hero, that he was saving her, when all along he'd just been manipulating her. "Vampire bastard!"

"Ah, love, now why are you so pissed at me?"

Her breath choked out and she whirled at the sound of his voice. He rose from the water, easily, fluidly, and the water slid over his powerful, bare chest. He was wearing a pair of pants, nothing more, and looking too damn sexy.

He's still controlling me.

She put her hands in front of her. "Stay away from me — and get *out* of my mind."

He shoved his fingers through his wet hair. Frowned at her. Advanced. "I haven't been in your mind. Just your body."

Asshole. He came closer. Closer —

She punched him.

Or, she tried to, anyway, but the vamp caught her fist in his hand and held her easily.

"Not quite the greeting I was expecting, not after last night."

Her cheeks burned. "What did you do to me?"

His thumb brushed lightly over her knuckles as he kept holding her hand prisoner. "Fucked you. I thought that was obvious."

Her other fist flew out. He caught it too. Shook his head. "Olivia, sweet Olivia..." He leaned in close toward her. "Don't you think it's a little soon to say we made love? I mean...it was rough and it was hot and it was fucking, so I don't know why you —"

"You used mind control on me."

His face hardened. "The hell I did." He still held both her hands in his grip.

"I don't...that wasn't *me*," she told him, frantic, her heart galloping too fast. So fast it hurt.

"Climaxed so long and hard you nearly drove me out of my head?"

How was this happening? "Let me go." Her voice was hoarse.

He hesitated.

"Let me go," she said again.

"Only if you promise not to punch me."

She nodded. Mentally crossed her fingers.

Slowly, he dropped her hands. "I didn't use mind control on you. You had sex with me because you wanted me." Anger roughened his words. "So maybe you're just having some morning after regret because you screwed a vamp, and you always thought you were better than that."

Better? No, that—

"We're good enough to be your lab rats, the experiments that you study so carefully, but you never thought you'd be begging one of us to take you."

Had she begged? She didn't remember that part, but a lot of the specific details about last night were kind of blurry.

This nightmare would never end.

Olivia retreated a bit, and her back bumped into the rocks. "You did something with your bite. You..."

"Made you climax?" He stalked closer, but didn't touch her again. "Because you did. You came—twice—just from my bite."

"You made me." The only explanation that made sense. "You compelled me—"

"If I could control you, I'd be doing it right now." Flat, brutal. Scary. "I'm not. I don't force women to do anything they don't want to do," he said with a barely banked fury. "Now I realize you've had some bad fucking hours at Purgatory, but watch your step, love. You don't want to push me too far."

She was trapped in a cave with a big, too-powerful vampire. Her fear was a living, breathing thing inside of her, but Olivia wasn't backing down. "Then what happened? If you didn't control me, *why* did I want you so much?"

He growled. "Because I'm dead fucking sexy?"

Her lips parted in surprise. But wait, yes, he was.

His hand lifted and skimmed down her cheek. Her racing heartbeat actually stopped in that moment. "Do you know what you are?" Shane asked her, his voice a rumble that sank beneath her skin.

Lost. Terrified. Mildly turned on. Olivia shook her head.

His finger slid down her throat. His thumb rubbed lightly over the spot he'd bitten the night before. Pleasure pulsed through her at that caress.

Maybe more than mildly turned on.

"You're a vampire's wet dream. A woman who craves the bite so much that it brings her to release." His hand tightened a bit around her throat. "No wonder you like to study the monsters so much. Deep down, you want us."

No, that wasn't true. Deep down, she was terrified of the monsters, but she did her job because there was no choice for Olivia. She *had* to do it.

I won't be like them.

His head began to lower toward hers.

"D-don't bite me again."

His eyes held hers. "Afraid you'll like it too much?"

Yes. "Just...don't." She also wanted his hand off her. Wanted his body away from her. The man's scent seemed to surround her, and her hands had clenched into fists because she was *not* going to touch him, even though part of her wanted to so very desperately.

It was the part that Olivia always kept chained up, locked deep inside of herself. The part that thrived on danger, that longed for the rush of wild, hot sex. The part that enjoyed the darkness...too much.

It was Olivia's secret side, a side that had terrified her for as long as she could remember.

It was a part that could be dangerous. Lethal.

Just like my father.

"Fine..." He smiled at her, and Olivia caught the glint of his fangs. "I'll keep my teeth away from your lovely throat, until you ask for my bite." He pulled away. Turned from her. Took two steps. Then glanced back. "And you *will* ask."

"Don't count on that." She wrapped her arms around her stomach.

"You liked the bite too much not to want it...me...again."

Her stomach clenched. "I just want to get out of here."

His gaze turned shuttered. "Is that what you truly wish? That you could leave Purgatory now?"

Coming there had been one serious mistake. "What I wish is that you'd tell me what's going on. Who you really are. What the hell is happening at this place. And yeah, after all that, I *wish* that we could get out of here. That we could just prance out of this cave and find a seaplane waiting to jet us to safety." She sucked in a ragged breath when she realized that her words were rapping out at a frantic pace. "That's what I wish, okay?"

He stared at her, then...shook his head, as if confused by her. "I told you...Pate sent me."

She stepped toward him. Her legs were all shaky and she could actually still *feel* the man inside of her. Inside. Outside. All around her. "You're FBI?"

He nodded.

"Since when does the FBI hire vampires?"

"Since I owed Eric Pate a blood debt, and this was my way of repaying him."

Oh...um, okay.

"I'm part of the Seattle Para Unit," he continued, his voice fully devoid of emotion. "When Pate's targets are too big for his normal resources to handle, I step in."

She ventured another step closer to him. "Shane Morgan...is that your real name?"

He shook his head, and her humiliation deepened. Wonderful. She'd had sex with a man without even knowing his real name.

"Shane Morgan is the name I use for my cover here at Purgatory. I've been Shane August. Shane Elliott, Shane—"

Olivia held up her hand. "I really get the idea." She stared at him. "What is your *real* name?"

"Just Shane is close enough. That's the name I've used the longest."

He was driving her crazy. "What's happening in Purgatory?"

"That's what I was supposed to find out." One blond brow lifted. "But then I got distracted by saving your sexy ass."

Did he think her ass was sexy? She almost glanced back but didn't. "Do you know a way for us to get off this island?" *That's it — just keep talking. Don't think about the sex or the bite. Just think about safety.*

"Maybe." His voice was mild. "But that's going to depend."

Another small step had her nearly touching him. "On what?"

His eyes narrowed. "On just how badly the people in Purgatory want you back."

The knots in her stomach were getting worse.

"I answered your questions, now you answer mine." He cocked his head. "Who sent you to Purgatory?"

Uh, they'd just covered this. "Pate. Eric Pate, you know —"

"Pate got orders from above that you were supposed to be shipped in. How'd you work that? *Who* sent you?"

Olivia shook her head.

"Don't play games with me." His face hardened as he stared at her. "If I'm risking my life for you, I want to know the risk is worth it. Because if you're playing me..."

"I'm not!"

"Then you'll pay." Flat. Cold.

"Look, I'm —"

He leapt toward her. Put his hand over her mouth and pulled her tightly against him.

She struggled, but he just held her tighter. She tried to —

A rock fell down from overhead, crashing against the side of the cave and ricocheting before it sank into the water. "They're close..." Shane whispered in her ear. His warning was a breath of sound. "Too close."

She couldn't hear anything but the desperate thunder of her heartbeat.

"Don't move."

His head slid back from her, and he glanced up. Another rock fell down, barely missing Olivia's foot.

She held herself perfectly still, too afraid in that instant to even breathe.

***

"They aren't here!" Case yelled at David. The werewolf was proving himself to be a total waste. They'd been all around the island, and the wolf had turned up *nothing* so far.

Case's head tilted back as he gazed at the water that surrounded the island. They were at the highest point on the island, a stony hill that gave them a vantage point to survey the area around them.

But we still haven't found the vampire.

"Alphas are supposed to be better than this," Case snarled. His fingers tightened around the collar's remote. Maybe it was time to find a new alpha to use on this hunt.

"In wolf form, I'd find them instantly." David's voice was low, tight with anger. "The wolf is always the stronger hunter."

Case frowned. He actually knew that bit was true, but... "You seriously think I'll let you take off that collar so you can change?" Did he look like an idiot?

David whirled toward him. "I'm close! I can catch the faintest hint of the vamp's scent...of *her*..." He shook his head. "But I won't get any closer, I won't find more unless I shift!"

Case shook his head and he hit the button on the remote—the button that would send a powerful surge of silver right into the werewolf's blood.

David gave a guttural cry of pain. "I...can...find them!"

"So can another wolf. One who doesn't have to shift in order to get the job done." He'd go through every werewolf in the place if he had to do it. Every single one.

Pain twisted the werewolf's face. "Others...can't...find them. Vamp was...smart. He went underwater...that-that cloaked...scent."

Yes, the vampire had been more resourceful than he'd expected, and Case still wanted to know how the vampire had known about the tunnel under Purgatory.

"The...only way...is if I shift..."

Case eased up on the remote and the silver concentration surging into David slowed. "You realize if I take off that collar, the only option for containing you will be death? If you make one wrong move, my men will be forced to pump you full of silver bullets."

Actually, the more he thought about it...

That idea works.

Case had planned to discard the werewolf, anyway. He couldn't let David go back and tell the others about the tunnel. Someone else might try to escape.

Not on my watch.

And if he were to spread the story that David had attacked his men or tried to flee, without his collar—*everyone will think his death was justified. The only recourse left to my men.*

"You won't have to...to contain me."

No, he wouldn't. Case would just kill him, *if* he had to do it. "Fine." Case nodded and motioned to his men. But they hesitated, and didn't move forward. "*Unlock his collar.*"

One guard began to inch toward David.

Case pulled out his gun. Checked the silver bullets. Then aimed the weapon at David. "One wrong move, and you're dead."

David nodded.

***

"We need to get out of here," Shane rasped. He'd caught the werewolf's scent, and that jerk David was far too close for his peace of mind.

With wide eyes, Olivia nodded. He saw her stare dip toward the water.

"Yes, love, sorry, but that's our only option." She was afraid of the water, he knew that. But better to face the water than a pissed-off werewolf. He caught her hand. Twined his fingers with hers. "It's all right. I've got you."

She bit her lip. The woman should *not* be doing that. When she nibbled that plump lower lip, it made him want to bite, and he'd just sprouted that BS about how he could easily hold off on biting her, how he'd wait for her to *ask* for his bite.

"Olivia..." Shane began, but then his head jerked to right at the distinct *popping* he'd just heard. A pop. A crack. A...growl. Every muscle in his body stiffened right then. No, oh, hell, no, that sound had better not be what he suspected it was.

"Shane?"

He heard the crack once more. "Bones are breaking." He hauled her toward the water. "That fool warden is letting the alpha shift."

"Y-you're saying a shifted werewolf is coming after us?"

They were at the edge of the water.

"He'll find us. Wherever we go on this island, the werewolf will find us." That was why they had to get off that island, right then. "You wished for the seaplane, right?"

"What?"

"*You want the seaplane.*" His fingers tightened on hers.

"Ouch! Yes, yes, I want the seaplane. I wish it was waiting for us. I want it—"

"Hold your breath."

She did.

They jumped into the water.

***

The change from man to beast was brutal. Vicious. Painful to see, and probably agony to feel.

Case kept his gun aimed at David as the werewolf shifted. The snapping and breaking of the wolf's bones seemed to go on forever, but in reality, he knew the transformation only lasted for a few moments. Just a few precious moments and then—

The shifted werewolf started clawing at the ground.

Case frowned at him. "What are you doing? You're supposed to find the vampire!"

The werewolf kept clawing, digging into the earth, digging down and down, as if he were trying to make a hole right beneath him.

Understanding hit Case. *Caves.* He'd heard there were a few caves scattered around the island, but they were only accessible from the sea.

And that vamp Shane had gone into the water when he'd fled Purgatory.

"Help him dig!" Case shouted to his men. "Help him!"

But then Case heard another sound on the horizon. At first, it was like the buzzing of a bee hive. But that sound grew louder, stronger.

No, no, not now!

He could just see the shape of the seaplane in the sky. Heading right toward them. That plane shouldn't have been there right then. There was no damn reason for the plane to come early. He fumbled for his radio and had to lower his gun. "Tell that pilot not to land! Get him out of here!"

As Case shouted, the werewolf's head turned toward him. Saliva dripped from the beast's mouth—a mouth bursting with razor sharp teeth.

The gun!

Case tried to aim his weapon once more, but the werewolf leapt for him. The beast's claws tore into Case's shirt. Blood soaked him. "Sh-shoot!" Case yelled as he tried to fight the werewolf.

The beast's teeth closed around his wrist. Sank in deep. Case cried out in pain.

Gunfire blasted.

The werewolf shuddered, jerked back, then raced away.

"After...him!" Case yelled as he tried to sit up. But the men didn't run after the werewolf. They crowded around him. "What the hell are you waiting for?" Case snarled. Blood pumped from the slashes in his chest and from the wound on his wrist.

"Sir..." One guard spoke, his voice little more than a whisper. "You've been...bitten."

He knew he had—he'd felt the werewolf's teeth tear into him.

"It's poison, sir," that guard continued. "Y-you know that."

Case shoved to his feet. Staggered.

"The bite either kills you...or changes you."

Case's blood covered fingers tightened around his gun. "I said...go after that bastard werewolf!" He took a step forward, and agony ripped through him.

The guards kept talking, but he couldn't hear them any longer. He was screaming because Case felt as if he were burning alive.

The bite either kills you...or changes you.

CHAPTER SIX

When she crawled up the beach, Olivia heard a low, droning *hum* sound. Her gaze jerked upward even as her fingers sank into the sand and she saw the seaplane heading toward them.

Relief had her shaking.

"Fucking figured…we are both screwed," Shane muttered as his hands closed around her hips and he hauled Olivia up to her feet.

"Screwed? We're saved!" She threw her arms around him and held on tight. "We're going to be all right! We're going—"

She heard a howl then. A long, angry howl from a wolf.

Shane lifted her into his arms in an instant, then he took off, moving with that vamp agility and speed, and she was so happy to be out of the water and heading toward the seaplane that she didn't even kick him for carrying her around like a sack of potatoes this time. He'd tossed her over his shoulder as he ran and she did her best to hold on as he rushed toward the droning/whirring sound of the seaplane's engine.

And the howls followed them. Howls and snarls that seemed to be getting so much closer.

"Stop!" A male's voice shouted. "Stop or I'll shoot!"

Shane staggered to a stop.

"Put the woman down."

She twisted around, trying to see who was shouting orders, and her gaze fell on the armed guards who were positioned at the edge of the dock. Five men stood there, weapons at the ready. Five men who blocked their escape because the seaplane was landing behind them, coming in with a spray of water.

Taking his time, Shane lowered Olivia to her feet.

"Come here, Dr. Maddox!" A blond guard shouted. "We'll keep you safe."

That wasn't just any blond guard. She recognized Evan. The man who'd left her with the wolves. And that jerk was offering her safety? Did she look like an idiot?

"Shane, it's him, he's the one who took me—"

Evan fired. The bullet flew through the air. Only the bullet wasn't aimed at Shane. It was aimed at her.

Shane leapt in front of her. The bullet thudded into his body. She heard the horrifying, sickening sound as it sank into him.

Then the other guards were firing. For an instant, the gunfire drowned out the approach of the plane. Olivia covered her ears, screaming because the bullets were all around them.

But the bullets didn't touch her. Shane was in front of her. Shielding her. Protecting her and—and then leaping for the guards when they stopped to reload.

He tore through them. All fangs and fury. Blood flowed, but this time, that blood came from the guards. Their bodies hit the ground as the men cried out in pain.

Her hands had fallen away from her ears. She stared at the men around her, but the scene seemed to flicker in her mind. The past and the present merged.

She saw another time. Another blood-soaked place.

Shane hadn't been there to shield her.

Her...her father had been there.

He'd laughed while he killed. *Laughed.* "*No one controls me!*" Her father's words were forever burned into her memory.

Her body shuddered.

The blood had splashed onto her when she'd been a child. It had covered her hands, her clothes. The blood —

"*Come on, Olivia!*" Shane roared, ripping her out of the past.

She blinked and realized that he was running down the narrow, wooden dock. Heading right toward the seaplane.

Shaking her head, she rushed after him. The men on the ground were still alive, she could hear their groans of pain. She darted around them, staying out of their reach, and hurrying toward the plane.

The pilot was still inside that seaplane. As Olivia watched, he shoved open his door and came out, armed.

"Shane, look out!"

But the pilot didn't aim his weapon at Shane. The tall, dark haired man's gaze flew toward her. Alarm flashed across his face. "*Hurry, run!*"

She *was* hurrying. It wasn't like she had vamp speed.

At the pilot's cry, Shane whipped back around toward her. She saw an expression of horror flash across his face.

Oh, no. If Shane was horrified, then whoever — whatever was behind her had to be very bad. Olivia ran as fast as she could. Shane was now leaping toward her and she wanted to get to that vampire because —

He can keep me safe.

Olivia risked a desperate glance over her shoulder. A werewolf was just feet away. A fully shifted, terrifying beast of a werewolf who was moving far too fast for her. The beast was easily twice the size of a normal wolf, and his thick fur was a stark white. Saliva dripped from his razor sharp teeth.

"*Get down!*" That bellow wasn't Shane's. Was it the pilot's? Didn't matter. Shane had just grabbed her wrist and pulled her against him even as more gunfire erupted.

But this time, the gunfire wasn't aimed at her or Shane. She peeked over her shoulder.

The werewolf had hit the ground. The bullets had hit him.

"Silver bullets, but I didn't hit his heart so *hurry the hell up!*"

Her head whipped back around. That was the pilot talking. The pilot who was frantically motioning toward them and telling Shane to, "Move the hell on, vamp!"

The pilot wasn't sounding the alarm? He was helping them?

Shane pretty much tossed her into that seaplane. He followed in right behind her.

"Damn nice timing, Connor," Shane muttered. "I owe you."

"You sure as hell do." The guy — Connor — was back in the pilot's seat. He was flipping dials and pushing some buttons and the plane was starting to move. "Now hold on, because we're going out fast and hot."

She held onto the seat with a death grip.

The plane sent water flying into the air as it pulled away from Purgatory, heading out toward the ocean, then going up and up.

Escape.

Olivia looked back at the island. The guards were still on the ground. And the werewolf was moving. Crawling toward...Evan? Yes, the guard was fumbling for his weapon but —

Her eyes squeezed shut when she heard his scream.

"Things on Purgatory are FUBAR," Shane said flatly.

She swallowed the lump in her throat.

"Get Pate. He needs to send men in there to take over right away," Shane continued, his voice a rumble that she could barely hear over the engines. "The warden's dirty, just like the last one, and whoever is pulling the strings on that place — whoever is in control back in D.C. — they want the paranormals on the edge out there."

She opened her eyes. Saw the waves beneath them.

"What the hell happened down there?" Connor demanded. "I got word from the boss that I needed to go in because he'd gotten Intel that some big powerhouse had come in at the island."

She turned her head. Found Shane watching her with eyes that seemed strangely cold. Suspicious.

"A powerhouse did come in," he agreed as he stared at Olivia. "But you can radio Pate and tell him that particular situation has been contained."

It had? From where she was sitting, nothing was contained at Purgatory.

"Tell him..." Shane continued as he reached over and grabbed a black bag. The pilot's bag? Shane pulled out a set of gleaming, silver hand-cuffs. "Tell him that I have her."

Her?

Then Shane grabbed her wrists. He locked the cuffs around her as she stared at him in shock.

"Pate needs to know that I've got a djinn."

"Are you crazy?" Olivia shrieked. But the plane was loud now, its engines whirling at full power. She could barely hear her own voice. "*What are you doing?*"

Even above the roar of the plane, she heard his clear and cold response, "Containing you."

***

"Take off the handcuffs, Shane."

The seaplane had just touched down off the Washington coast. It wasn't a location that saw much air traffic—in fact, Shane would guess that the rickety dock didn't see much traffic at all.

"I know you heard me. Take them *off*."

Connor killed the engines. He glanced back at them, one brow raised. "I think we both heard you, Dr. Maddox, but if Shane says you need to be contained..." His golden eyes narrowed on her. Obviously, he thought she was a threat. "You're being contained."

Her mouth opened, closed, then opened again. Her cheeks were flushed, and her eyes gleamed. "This isn't happening, I wish you would—"

Shane hated to do it. Oh, damn, he hated it, but he gagged her then.

Fear flashed across her face when he tied the small rope behind her head. He'd moved so fast that she hadn't been given the chance to fight him.

"Uh, yeah..." Connor's voice was guarded. "When are you going to update me on what's going on with her?"

"Soon," he promised. As soon as he had her calm and—

Olivia tried to head-butt him. And for the fifth time, the fifth damn time, he attempted to use compulsion on her.

When a vampire drank from a human, a link was formed. The vampire could control his prey. And that link of control wasn't just exclusive to humans, either. Vamps could control werewolves the same way. They were supposed to be able to control *all* prey.

But he couldn't forge any kind of link with her.

They'd radioed Pate on the way there, told him to lock down Purgatory as fast as he could, and updated the boss about Olivia. After he'd sworn to hell and back, Pate had given them directions to this safe house. Just beyond the dock, Shane could see the faded cabin that waited. He could also see the man striding from that cabin—Eric Pate looked pissed.

Shane felt the same way.

"We aren't going to hurt you," Shane told Olivia, and he hoped those words were true. They'd have to interrogate her, have to discover all of the secrets that the woman might not even realize she possessed.

She was dangerous, a threat that couldn't be ignored. Someone in power had arranged for her to visit Purgatory because that *someone* knew exactly what Olivia was.

In the wrong hands, Olivia could prove to be more than lethal.

She could prove to be fucking Armageddon.

Connor exited the seaplane. Keeping his hold on Olivia, Shane followed. She dug in her heels, she growled behind the gag, and he was pretty sure those growls translated to "Asshole" or "Bastard" and he thought there was a "Burn in hell" thrown in there, too.

"Already been there," he told her as he pulled her along the dock. "It wasn't nearly as hot as you'd expect."

The growled/muffled version of "Asshole" came again.

Pate waited for them at the end of the dock. The wind blew against his hair and sent his coat flapping back, clearly revealing the gun strapped to his hip. Pate had his arms crossed over his chest. As Shane approached him, Pate gave a sad shake of his head. "This wasn't the way the mission was supposed to end."

"Yes, well, then maybe you shouldn't have Ok'ed the entrance of a djinn into Purgatory."

More muffled grunts came from Olivia.

"I didn't realize that she *was* a djinn, not when I sent her in." His words sounded disgusted. "Now that I know…you'll see that things have changed. I dug up every bit of research I had on djinns. We *can* contain her."

Olivia went silent.

"Fuck me," Pate muttered, "this isn't going to be easy." His gaze swept around the area. "Hide the plane, Connor, then come inside for the interrogation."

Olivia's whole body stiffened at the word "interrogation."

Pate stared at her with hard eyes. Shane had seen that expression on his friend's face before. It was Pate's I'll-Do-Anything-Necessary look. Shit.

"Bring her." Then Pate turned and headed back toward the cabin.

Shane glanced at Olivia. She shook her head, frantic.

His jaw locked. "You don't understand how many lives are on the line here."

A tear leaked down her cheek, and the sight of that lone tear did something to him. His chest ached, and Shane found himself leaning toward her. Brushing that tear away, then letting his fingers linger against her cheek. "I'll protect you."

He *hadn't* meant to reveal that. Hell, the addiction was worse than he'd thought.

Using his hold on her hand-cuffs, he pulled her toward the cabin. As soon as he got inside and smelled the incense, he knew Pate had been busy. A quick glance at the floor showed the old, intricate symbols that had been painted there, and the familiar scent told Shane that his friend had used blood to make those marks.

A chair sat in the middle of the markings.

Olivia squirmed in his grip, but Shane pushed her toward the chair. In a lightning-fast move, he unhooked her cuffs. She was sighing with relief when he quickly grabbed her arms again and re-cuffed her. Only this time, the cuffs were behind her back.

She mumbled behind her gag and—

He used a knife to cut the gag away.

"You bastard!" Olivia heaved out. Then she blinked and seemed to realize that the gag was gone. "Help! Someone, help me!"

Pate shut the cabin's door. "There's no one here to help you."

Her gaze was on Shane. *Help me.* It was too easy to read the desperate plea in her eyes.

He tossed away the gag. Put the knife back on the table with the...other instruments that Pate had out. His gaze lingered on that instrument tray. He'd seen paranormal interrogations before, and he knew just how intense they could become.

I can't let that happen to her.

He put his body in front of Olivia and turned to face Pate. His friend. The man he might have to attack in a few moments. "You have a holding spell in place."

"Damn straight I do. If she really is a djinn, her wishes won't work here." Pate's lips twisted. "For a little while, anyway."

"I'm not a djinn!" Olivia shouted.

Pate paced around the room. "Tell me more about what went down on Purgatory." The words were calm, but an angry tension hung in the air around Pate. "That place is a powder keg, and the last thing I want is for it to explode."

Shane exhaled on a ragged breath. "Too late. I'd say an explosion is imminent."

Pate swore. "I've already got a dozen of my agents en route to contain the place. I've got—"

"A guard took her to the werewolves." He waved his hand behind him to indicate a glaring Olivia. "And he left her there with them." Anger rushed through him when he remembered her fear. "I almost didn't get to her in time."

Pate's eyes widened a bit. "All of the guards were supposed to be replaced at Purgatory. New guards, new warden. They were handpicked—"

"By you?" Shane demanded as he felt his fangs burn in his mouth. He'd always trusted Pate, from the first time that he'd seen the guy in that burning desert in the Middle East, but if Pate was turning on him...

"Hell, no, not by me. I don't manage Purgatory. I run the Para Unit." His jaw locked. "We catch the beasts. Someone else keeps them caged."

"That someone is doing a piss-poor job."

"Uh, hello?" Olivia demanded. The chair's legs slammed to the floor beneath her heaving, bouncing body. "Could you please do something about the woman you've got *handcuffed* here!"

Pate and Shane spun to face her.

She leveled her furious stare on Pate. "You've got problems at Purgatory, big ones, okay? I was supposed to interview werewolves, and they gave me a silver remote that wouldn't even work on them!" Olivia frantically shook her head. "Then, yes, the guard—Evan—just took me to the werewolves. The werewolves in *maximum security*. He threw me in there with them and…and just left me."

A snarl built in Pate's throat. He slanted a hard glance at Shane. "And where is this Evan now?"

"The last I saw of him," Shane said softly, "a fully shifted werewolf was going for his throat."

"*Shifted?*"

"The warden was letting the wolf track me and Olivia. The fool took the werewolf's collar off."

"That's against every protocol they have at Purgatory." Pate started his frantic pacing again.

"Yes, well…" Shane jerked a hand through his hair. "Protocol isn't big there. The place is still out of control. I don't know what bull you're being fed, but it's chaos there."

Pate yanked out his phone. Marched for the door. "My men will take over. They'll secure the place."

Shane tilted his head as he studied Pate's retreating figure. "Who's responsible for caging them?"

Pate glanced back at him. "Senator Donald Quick, the man who *guaranteed* that Purgatory would not fail this time."

Is he the man you believe is setting us all up for disaster?

Pate's stare darted back to Olivia. "I'll be right back, Dr. Maddox, and when I return, you *will* tell us your secrets."

"I'm the victim here!" Olivia yelled at him.

Pate grunted and left the cabin. The door shut softly behind him.

"This is insane." Her breathless voice had Shane glancing at her again. "Uncuff me. Stop this madness right now!"

He wanted to but... "There are two ways this can work." She shook her head.

"You can tell us what we want to know. Start talking now, on your own..." He closed in on her. Shane leaned close to Olivia. Her sensual scent wrapped around him. "Or we make you talk."

Fear flashed in her beautiful eyes. He hated that look of fear. Hated that he was the cause of her terror.

"I thought you were protecting me," she whispered as she gave a confused shake of her head. "Why are you doing this?"

He leaned in even closer. Close enough to kiss her. And he could still taste her on his tongue. "Because you're a weapon that can be used to hurt a lot of people. I can't let that happen." He'd seen too much death, too many slaughters in all of his centuries.

"I'm not a weapon." She shook her head once more. Her hair slid over her shoulders. "I'm just a person." Her voice lowered to a desperate, husky rasp, "Please, Shane, don't do this to me. I-I'm scared."

His gut clenched. "Just talk, Olivia. Tell us what we need to know!"

She jerked and the chair bounced on its legs. "There's nothing to tell! I'm a normal woman, I'm not some – some djinn! I thought you were helping me!" Now her voice wasn't a whisper, it was closer to a yell. "But you're playing some game that I don't understand!"

His hands closed around her delicate shoulders. He pushed down, stopping her frantic movements. "Why are you drawn to monsters?"

"What?"

"Human killers. Paranormal killers. Why do they fascinate you so much?"

Her eyelashes flickered. "Because I want to stop them. I-I don't want anyone else to get hurt—"

He brought his mouth next to her ear. "You're lying to me," he murmured. "Don't do that. Not again."

The scent of her fear deepened.

He pulled back. Stared into her eyes once more. "Why do you like the monsters?"

She shook her head.

"*Why*, Olivia?"

"I don't like monsters!"

He nodded even as a cold dread slid through him. "So you're choosing option two?"

The door creaked open behind him. Footsteps padded into the room. He glanced back and saw both Pate and Connor enter the room.

"The Para Unit will take over Purgatory. My men will stand guard until *I* say otherwise," Pate told him flatly. "Provided, of course, they get there and the whole place isn't already a bloodbath."

Shane was sure there would be plenty of blood on the ground at Purgatory.

Pate's brow lifted as his stare shifted to Shane's hands — and their hold on Olivia's shoulders. "Are you ready to talk, Dr. Maddox?"

"I don't have anything new to say! I was sent to do research — you okayed my trip there! You're the one who sent me!"

Pate shook his head. "I didn't want to send you there. I wasn't given much of a choice. Again…" His gaze darted to Shane. "The senator was using his pull. Senator Quick wanted to make sure that humane conditions were being maintained at the facility. Getting a shrink in there for the inmates…that was his brilliant idea."

Connor propped his back against a nearby wall. Both his brows climbed as he said, "And the senator wanted her to be the one going in?"

Pate rubbed his jaw. "She was the one directly recommended by Quick. The senator said she was already well acquainted with paranormals, and when I interviewed her, she backed that up." His gaze narrowed on Olivia. "You said you knew all about the monsters out there."

Shane forced himself to release Olivia's shoulders.

"Just how well acquainted are you?" Pate asked Olivia.

Her breath blew out in a hard rush. "The senator...I've known him for years. He helped me get some grants that I used with my research—"

"That tells me nothing about your relationship with other paranormals." Pate's voice was flat.

"I-I don't have a relationship with other paranormals."

Pate glanced at Connor, then back at Shane. Finally, his considering gaze returned to Olivia. "How did you learn of the existence of paranormals? That little bit wasn't in your file, though I am starting to realize that file of yours...data in it was no doubt faked. Perhaps by your friend, the senator."

Olivia licked her lips. "I saw werewolves attack when I was a teenager, okay? Th-the senator's daughter, Chloe, she and I went to school together. We were friends."

Pate waited.

"We were walking home together one night when the werewolves attacked. It was a pack of them, and they closed in on us as we screamed."

Shane's teeth were fully extended in his mouth. *Fucking werewolves...*

"You weren't bitten," Pate said as he studied her with avid interest. "Obviously."

"No." Voice softer, she said, "I wasn't."

"And I've never heard anything about the senator's daughter being a werewolf."

Olivia's mouth closed. Because Shane was watching her so closely, he saw the faint flicker of her eyelashes.

And Pate must have seen that telling movement too, because he pounced and asked, "*Is* Chloe Quick a werewolf?"

Olivia just stared at him.

A long sigh slipped from Pate. "You are making this too hard."

"Chloe Quick is my friend."

Pate circled around her, like a lion, closing in on his prey. Shane didn't move.

"You want to find out why monsters attack..." Pate mused. "The senator is supporting you, giving you upclose and personal access to the monsters. Why? Why is he doing that? Is it because you *both* want to help Chloe? She's changed, she can't control her beast, and you're trying to save her?"

"Chloe doesn't need saving," she said softly.

"*Who does?*"

Olivia jerked back against the chair. "We all do. My research can help so—"

"I'm done with this." Pate waved his hands in disgust. "I don't have time to waste this way." He nodded toward Shane. "Bite her. Make her talk."

"No!" Olivia's desperate cry. Her gaze jerked to him. "Shane, *no!*"

"Do it, Shane," Pate said. "Then you can make her tell us what we need to know."

That was the way things were *supposed* to work. But this wasn't a typical situation. "My bite doesn't work on her."

"What?" Shock was clear on Pate's face.

Shane brushed back Olivia's hair, revealing the faint marks he'd left on her neck. *His* marks. "Controlling her that way isn't an option."

The room got very, very quiet then. Shane knew Pate was absorbing the full magnitude of this revelation. As ancient as Shane was, he should have been able to control anyone or anything.

There were only a handful of vampires who could claim to be older than Shane. And with the vamps, age brought power.

"A djinn," Pate said. "Sonofabitch, I didn't want that shit to be true." Then he turned and reached for the instrument table. He picked up the knife. "I guess we have to do this the hard way."

"St-stop!" Olivia shouted.

"Pate..." Connor began, a nervous edge in his voice.

"I've never met a djinn. The last one was supposed to have been killed about twenty years ago, after he went on a killing spree and took the lives of everyone in his path. Humans. Werewolves. Vampires."

Olivia shook her head. "I'm not...*I'm not!*"

Pate was staring down at the gleaming edge of that silver knife. "If she's a djinn, we have to bind her power so she can't hurt anyone."

"I'm not hurting anyone!"

Pate advanced with his knife.

"Stop it!" Olivia shouted again. "I'm not some genie! I don't live in a bottle! I don't grant wishes!"

The knife was getting close to her. Pate was less than a foot away. "That's not how it works," Pate told her softly. "Real djinns are dark, governed by need and passion. They like the surge of wild power that fills them every time they use their magic. Lives don't matter to them."

"That isn't me!"

"There is no bottle to bind you. Your powers are controlled another way. Blood and fire."

Her breath was coming in fast, frantic heaves. Shane could see the shudder of her chest.

"If you control a djinn, you have enormous strength. The djinn can grant your wishes. Give you anything and everything you want. Your every heart's desire."

The knife was held easily in his hand.

"Or the djinn can twist your desires," Pate murmured, a dark edge in those words. "Turn your wishes and dreams into nightmares."

"Shane..." Olivia's gaze locked on his. "Help me! Please!"

"No one can help you now," Pate told her, "not if you really are a djinn." And he lunged forward with the knife.

CHAPTER SEVEN

Olivia screamed and turned her head to the side because she didn't want to see that knife coming at her. She expected to feel the blade slicing across her skin. Expected to feel the white-hot pain as it sank into her.

Instead, she heard…a pained grunt. The clatter of something falling onto the floor.

The thud of flesh hitting flesh.

She cracked open one eye and turned her head.

Then she cracked open both eyes.

The knife was on the floor.

Pate was pinned to the wall by a seriously enraged looking Shane, and the other guy—Connor—was trying to pull Shane off his prey.

She twisted her wrists, jerking and pulling, trying to break free of the cuffs so she could get out of there while she had the chance.

"Let him go, Shane!" Connor snarled.

Shane tightened his hold on Pate's neck. "You *never* hurt her! You don't go after her with your knife! She's *mine!*"

That deafening roar pretty much terrified Olivia. She jerked again at the cuffs, but she wound up falling and her chair crashed to the floor. At that sound, all of the men turned to stare at her.

Her gaze met Shane's. Her terror doubled right then, because the man he'd been before was gone. The vampire was fully ruling him in that moment. She could see it. His eyes had darkened with power. His teeth were fully extended and wicked sharp.

The chair had broken beneath her. She scrambled to her feet and made a mad dash for the door—

Except she didn't get to the door. She got right to the edge of those strange markings on the floor, and it was as if she'd just slammed into some kind of invisible wall.

"Not...going...anyplace..." Pate gasped out. "Djinn!"

The cuffs bit into her wrists. Her hands were still behind her back, and those cuffs seemed to hurt her more with every second that passed. "What's happening?" There was nothing there, nothing she could see, but Olivia was trapped.

The past rose around her again. She could see the blood. Hear the screams...

But I can't get to them. I'm trapped. Trapped!

Shane let go of Pate. Shane's glittering, too dark eyes were on her. Hungry. Possessive.

"Welcome..." Pate said, his voice stronger, "to your bottle, djinn."

***

Connor dragged Shane out of the cabin, and a still wheezing Pate followed them. Pate slammed the door shut behind him, then he glared at Shane. "What the fuck was that? I was just going to nick her a little because I needed her blood!"

Shane tried to pull back his control, but it was gone. He kept seeing Olivia. Her fear. Smelling her fear. Hearing her pleading voice.

Shane...Help me! Please!

"Mine now..." He barely recognized his own guttural voice.

"Oh, shit." Pate shoved him hard. "Just how much blood did you drink from her?"

Not enough.

"Yeah…" Connor drawled as he put his hands—claw-tipped hands—on his hips. "Somebody needs to explain to me just what the hell is going on. One minute, I think I'm rescuing a human, the next thing I know, we're imprisoning a genie? *A genie?*"

Shane's gaze returned to the cabin's door. He took a step toward that door. Toward Olivia.

Pate shoved him back once more. A shove too strong for a human, but then, Shane knew all too well that Pate wasn't as mortal as he pretended to be. "Get your control back!" Pate snapped.

Shane bared his fangs at the man. "*Never* come at her with a knife."

Pate's eyes closed. "She's messing with your mind. I heard that her kind might be able to do that. Blur reality. Get you to see and feel what she wants…" His eyes opened, and Pate pointed to the dock. "Go for a long walk, vamp. Find someone in the next town to drink. Get some space from her, and you'll get your control back."

He didn't want control. He wanted Olivia.

A twig snapped as Connor advanced on them. "I'm still waiting for an explanation."

"And I'm trying to stop him from tearing us both apart!" Pate threw back.

Shane was definitely in the mood for a fight.

"Walk it off," Pate advised him, and his eyes flashed then. Not deepening like a vampire's, but swirling with colors. "Walk. It. Off. Go find someone else to bite."

And he did want to bite. Fury and bloodlust tangled within him. The fury had risen so suddenly, so strongly when Pate had actually gone toward Olivia—everything had altered in that instant. He took a step toward the cabin, but found Connor blocking his path.

"You heard the boss," Connor muttered.

"Not *my* boss…" Shane threw back. Time to stop playing games. As far as he was concerned, he'd paid his blood debt to Pate. More than paid that shit. "Move." A warning. Either the werewolf moved from his path or Shane would be moving him.

"Don't you see?" Pate asked him. "This isn't you! This is what a djinn can do! They are born of darkness, bound to the dark always. She'll twist your emotions. Make you turn on your friends."

He hesitated. Shane knew the emotions he was feeling weren't normal. Back at that cabin, he'd been seconds away from ripping out Pate's throat.

He tried to hurt Olivia.

A growl broke from Shane.

"That's why the djinns were killed instead of revered. They were too dangerous. They're dark, evil at their core."

Shane shook his head. That wasn't Olivia. She wasn't evil.

Sanity tried to push through his rage. He attempted to piece this puzzle together and he spoke slowly, "She…doesn't know."

Correction, she *hadn't* known.

He sucked in a deep breath. Another. Forced himself to turn away from that cabin. To take a few steps away.

"Are you coming back to us?" Pate asked him softly.

Shane managed a jerky nod.

And he took a few more steps away from the cabin.

"Her desperation must have done it." Pate sounded as if he were figuring out a puzzle, too. "She's got you in her web, and her panic hit you."

No, her panic and fear had enraged him. Shane jerked a hand over his face. He could still feel Olivia's pull. He wanted to go back in that cabin and be with her. "She…didn't know." Of this, he was sure. "Not…before Purgatory."

Pate's expression was calculating. "Then someone suspected what she was. What better place to push out her darkness than in the middle of Purgatory?"

Someone had sent Olivia to the wolves. Literally. "The senator…"

"If he knew what she was…or suspected…Purgatory would be the perfect place to break her."

Shane's hands were fisted at his sides.

"If the werewolves in Purgatory had control of a djinn," Pate said softly, "just what do you think they'd do with her?"

Use her to destroy. He swallowed, tasting the ash of fury on his tongue. "Is a djinn really that powerful?" Because he'd never come across one, not in all of his many, many centuries.

"Civilizations are said to have fallen because of them."

He shook his head.

"Fuck," Connor's voice was a rough rasp. "Maybe you should have led with that Intel, boss."

"They were all supposed to be dead." Pate started to pace. "I know because I damn well read the files that the FBI had on them. Twenty years ago, they were hunted to extinction. The last djinn went out in a fury of fire and blood."

Connor whistled. "So what the hell are we supposed to do with her?"

Shane's head turned toward the cabin. He could hear the faint sound of crying from inside that cabin. Crying and…

His name.

She was whispering his name.

Shane took three fast steps toward her. Both Connor and Pate jumped in his path. "You need distance, buddy," Pate told him quietly. "Distance and someone else's blood." He huffed out a breath. "Look, Holly is already en route, okay? She'll run some tests on Dr. Maddox and find out exactly what we're dealing with here."

Holly. Shane knew the guy was talking about Dr. Holly Young, a physician *and* vampire who treated the members of Pate's Para Unit. Holly was also Pate's step-sister.

"You trust Holly. You know she won't hurt Dr. Maddox."

No, Holly wouldn't. Because Holly had been through her own hell and survived.

Pate slanted a glance toward Connor. "Your brother will be coming with her."

Connor's expression hardened. "Wherever she goes, he's never far behind."

Damn straight, Duncan McGuire wasn't. The guy was mated to Holly. Once a werewolf, Duncan had become something a whole lot more dangerous thanks to his connection with Holly.

"We've got this," Pate assured Shane. "Now go and try to dilute the blood you took — get her out of your system."

He turned away. Took one step. Another.

"Out of curiosity…" Pate's voice was halting. "What happened when you bit Dr. Maddox?"

She came for me. I got addicted to her.

Instead of answering, Shane amped up his speed and left that cabin in his dust.

***

She was on her knees when the door opened. Olivia's hair had fallen over her face and she tilted her head back so that she could see who'd come to torment her now.

It was the dark-haired man who'd piloted the seaplane. Connor. He shut the door then leaned back against it, staring at her with a hooded gaze. The gold of his stare seemed far too deep, too dark.

"You know…" Olivia had to clear her throat. "I was actually glad to see you back at Purgatory." She rose to her feet. Her knees only trembled a little. "Now…not so much."

His lips quirked a bit. Then he glanced around the area. Her little prison. *My bottle?* She'd grabbed the broken chair with her cuffed hands and smashed it against her invisible walls. The chair had gone straight through.

Olivia hadn't.

"You don't look so dangerous," Connor told her.

"Neither do you," Olivia threw right back. Obviously that was the *wrong* thing to say because in the next instant, claws burst from his fingertips.

Werewolf.

"Don't underestimate me," he warned her.

So he was far more dangerous than he'd appeared at first glance.

She jumped back a few feet. "Why is the FBI hiring werewolves?"

"Because we can get the job done for Uncle Sam. We can track the killers." His too-sharp teeth snapped together. "And we can stop them." He took a step forward and she automatically retreated. Connor shook his head. "What's wrong, doctor? I thought you liked interviewing your monsters."

But she hadn't been the prisoner during those interviews. She was now. "A week ago, I was teaching a criminal psychology class to freshmen at Wellswright University. Now I'm...here." She looked down at the markings on the floor. Markings that held her prisoner. Markings that assured her this was no nightmare. This was real.

"Someone's coming to study you."

Her head whipped up at that bit of news.

"A physician will be here soon. She's going to take your blood. Analyze your DNA. Then we'll have conclusive proof about what you are and what you're not."

Human.

Her skin seemed to itch then, as if — as if something were moving within her. She'd felt too hot for the last few moments. Too scared. "You all think I'm being used, don't you? That I was sent to Purgatory as some kind of power play?"

He advanced toward her, but didn't cross the markings. "I think you're a pawn." There was pity in his golden eyes. "I think you had no clue what the hell you were, last week, when you were teaching those freshmen. And I think your world has been wrecked around you."

He felt sorry for her. Maybe she could use that. Maybe she could use him. "I didn't ask for any of this."

"We never do." Pain flashed, swallowing the pity in his gaze. "But we still have to live with what happens to us."

Her eyes swept over him. This man—this werewolf—was close to Shane's size. His shoulders were broad, his arms muscled. Where Shane was classically handsome, Connor's face was harder. Rougher. Stubble lined his jaw and his eyes blazed with emotion.

"They're going to dig into your life," Connor told her. "Learn every secret that you ever kept. They won't stop until they discover everything, and then, they're going to give you a choice. Except it won't be a choice, not really. You'll either work with Pate or..."

And he didn't finish.

She swallowed the lump that wanted to choke her. "How do you know?"

"Because that's what they did to me."

There was a ring of truth to his words that she couldn't deny.

"I've been *in* Purgatory, as a prisoner." His jaw locked. "And let's just say I would have done anything to make sure I didn't get caged again."

Her shoulders were aching. The cuffs were still behind her back and she hurt. "Will you uncuff me?"

"The Para Unit uses those specifically to restrain the stronger paranormals."

The stronger paranormals.

"The more you struggle against them, the tighter they'll become."

"That tidbit would have been helpful sooner," she muttered as Olivia tried to relax and not struggle any more. That was a whole lot of too little, too late, and her aching muscles needed relief.

Her gaze slid behind Connor. "Is…is Shane outside?"

"No." Clipped.

Did his short response mean that sharing time was over? "Where is he?"

"He left."

That answer shouldn't have hurt. It did. "He…left me?"

Connor stared back at her. "He was shot several times back at Purgatory. He healed, but he needed blood to get his strength back up."

Oh. So he'd gone to feed on someone.

Her cheeks flamed as she remembered what had occurred when he bit *her*. Then her stomach knotted as she realized that he was out there, and probably getting ready to sink his teeth into some other woman.

She spun on her heel, giving the wolf her back.

Olivia tried to take in deep, even breaths but her fear and fury were pumping together within her. "I guess he's not drinking from a blood bag." Really, would that have been too much to ask?

"No, he's not."

She flexed her fingers. "I can't feel them, you know."

Silence.

Olivia looked back at Connor. "I've lost all sensation in my fingers. I get that these cuffs are used on the paranormals. On the vampires. On the werewolves." She paused a beat. That flash of pity had been real in his eyes before. Maybe she *could* use it. "But I'm not a werewolf. Or a vampire. These cuffs are hurting me, and I-I'm afraid…" The tremble in her voice wasn't faked. "It's too tight. I can't see my fingers, but are they…are they starting to discolor?"

He inched closer.

"They are, aren't they? Please, just loosen them for me. I don't want to lose my hands."

Slowly, he reached into his pocket and pulled out a small set of keys.

Her breath rushed out. "Thank you."

***

Her blood, her skin, her taste...

"Uh, is something wrong?" The woman before Shane asked, frowning up at him. She was a pretty blonde. A pretty blonde who'd been flirting with him from the moment he entered the diner. She leaned toward him, showing off a very ample bosom. "Is there something I can do for you?"

He'd taken blood too many times to count. He knew how to seduce in order to get exactly what he wanted.

He should smile at the woman. Feed her a line. Get her to walk outside with him. Then he'd find a secluded spot and feed on her.

Except...

Her scent was wrong.

Her voice was wrong.

Her hair was wrong.

She was wrong.

Shane wanted blood, all right, but not that woman's. He hungered, he needed, but he didn't need her.

Oh, hell, I am so screwed. Because he realized what was happening. He'd seen this same twisted shit go down before.

Growling, he spun away from the blonde. Marched back outside. The sun was still shining. Most vamps would have been hiding in the shadows right then. He wasn't most vamps. He glared up at the sun.

And went back — almost helplessly — to *her*.

***

His fingers slid over her wrists. "Dammit, you did a number on yourself," Connor muttered.

Olivia rolled her eyes. Right. Because she'd cuffed herself. The injury was totally her fault — *not*. "You guys should have told me that the cuffs tightened automatically. At first, I thought I was just dreaming that crap." There was a soft snick behind her. Then finally, finally, the cuffs were falling away. Wonderful. Fantastic —

Pain.

She moaned as the feeling came back to her fingertips and that feeling was burning pain.

"Easy." His slightly rough fingers began to stroke her hands. "I'll help you."

She looked down at the floor. He'd crossed the red markings on the floor in order to reach her, but he'd been careful not to smudge those strange lines. If she could catch him off-guard, maybe Olivia could shove him back and make him fall onto the marks — perhaps she could get out then.

I've been trapped like this before.

The knowledge was there, but she couldn't pull it out from the depths of her mind. No matter how hard she tried, she just couldn't remember when she'd been held prisoner like this.

Blood and fire.

"Genies grant wishes, don't they?" Connor asked. His fingers were still rubbing her wrists, her hands.

She didn't reply. She had no clue what genies were supposed to do. Olivia was too busy trying to figure out how to get away from him.

"I have a wish." His head was bent toward her. He seemed to surround her, and a shiver slid over Olivia.

The werewolf is dangerous.

"I wish that I weren't so fucking twisted on the inside."

His gruff words catapulted her into action. She whirled around, and even though he was bigger and stronger, she was the desperate one. Olivia heaved against him. Sure enough, he stumbled back, and his booted feet slipped over the markings, smudging them.

Work, work, work —

She leapt forward, lunging across those smudged markings, and the invisible wall didn't slap her back down. Euphoria burst through her as Olivia rushed for the door.

But a hard hand grabbed her ankle and yanked her back. She hit the floor and then he was on her. Connor grabbed her hands. Pinned them above her. His eyes were blazing — glowing with the familiar stare of a werewolf and then darkening with — with the power of a vampire?

Impossible!

"Help!"

His fangs were out.

The door flew open behind them and thudded into the wall. Then Connor was ripped off her. Tossed across the room by an enraged Shane. And Shane didn't stop there. He flew after Connor, heading in with powerful fists and bared fangs.

Olivia staggered to her feet, then she ran out of that door. She didn't see Pate, didn't see anyone, and her gaze flew around frantically as she tried to find some way to escape from that area.

Light glinted off something to the right — *something…*she rushed forward. Yanked back a tarp and saw that the light had been shining off a motorcycle's handlebars. Her hands searched all over the motorcycle as she chanted, "Key, key, key —"

"*Olivia!*"

Uh, oh. That bellow had to be Shane's.

But even as that bellow echoed around her, Olivia's fingers curled around the key. She had that motorcycle roaring to life two seconds later and she wobbled on the thing as she tried to steady it and get away.

"Olivia, no!"

She'd never ridden a motorcycle in her life, and the one she was on seemed freaking huge as she tried to steady it. She was struggling with the clutch and what she thought was the throttle, or maybe it was the gear shifter and —

Pate appeared in front of her. About twenty feet away. He had his gun up and aimed at her.

She was heading right for him. Olivia jerked the handlebars to the right, and that was when she lost her barely-there control on the motorcycle. The wheels spun. Gravel flew, and the motorcycle careened toward a tree.

Before the impact, the last thing she heard was Shane shouting her name.

CHAPTER EIGHT

"Come on, Olivia, open your eyes for me."

The voice was familiar, tempting. Her eyelashes lifted, slowly, and the room around her came into focus.

"That's better." Shane leaned over her. Worry had etched a faint line between his brows. "How do you feel?"

"Like I hit a tree."

A faint laugh came from the corner of the room. Her gaze slid over there, and a rough pounding shot through her temples.

A man stood in the shadows, a guy Olivia was pretty sure she hadn't seen before. His blue eyes swept over her. "I think that's because you *did* hit a tree, Dr. Maddox."

With his words, her failed escape attempt came rushing back to her. Olivia tried to sit up in bed, but Shane's hands came down, and he held her in place. "Easy. You've been out for hours."

Out? That would explain the throbbing head.

"Do you always heal so quickly, Dr. Maddox?" The man in the corner asked her.

She didn't feel like she'd healed. She felt like she had a concussion. "I don't exactly crash into trees a lot, so I'm not real sure about that." Her speech wasn't slurred. That had to be a plus.

"If you'd watched those deep wounds heal, the way we did, you *would* be sure."

What was that guy talking about?

Shane's fingers stroked over her shoulders. At the unexpected caress, her attention slid right back to him. He didn't look like a wild, out of control vampire as he leaned over her. He looked...

Worried. Protective.

How very human of him.

"No more handcuffs?" she whispered to Shane.

He shook his head.

"And I guess you had a nice, big meal before coming back, huh?" Wait, Olivia hadn't meant to say that and she definitely hadn't meant for the words to come out with a jealous edge.

Shane frowned down at her. "I haven't fed yet." He paused. His gaze heated. "Are you offering?"

"I—*no*." Yes.

The door opened then, and a woman with dark hair bustled inside. The woman was looking down at a chart as she entered the room. "I'm running her blood work now. Man, it's amazing the way Pate had that remote lab set up here. I bet I could even do a bone marrow analysis—"

"No, you couldn't," Olivia said flatly.

The woman jerked to a stop. Her brown eyes were wide with surprise as she said, "You're awake."

Yes, she was, *obviously*, and since the woman was talking about bone marrow work, Olivia knew she had to be staring at the doctor Connor had mentioned to her before.

Olivia's gaze slid to her arm. A small bandage covered a patch of skin on her inner wrist. But that was the only bandage she saw. That other guy must have been bullshitting about her "deep wounds" healing. She didn't have other injuries. That was all.

Am I lying to myself?

She...was. But others had lied to her, too.

Her stare rose. Fixed on Shane. "You gave them my blood." And it felt like a betrayal.

He flushed. "We're trying to understand you."

"And I'm trying to understand how my life has turned into such a nightmare!"

Pate joined their little party. Perfect. He strode in as if he owned the place. *Oh, wait...he does.*

"I told you," Pate said, his voice low and rumbling, "I didn't think you were prepared for Purgatory."

Shane's fingers stroked over her arm once more.

Olivia took a good look around then. She was back in the cabin. Unfortunately. They'd pulled a bed into the center of those red markings—markings that were fully intact once again. Her bottle.

"If I were a genie," she said—genie, djinn—whatever, "don't you think I would have realized that fact by this point in my life?"

"I don't know." It was the other woman who answered. Olivia couldn't remember the chick's name. "Have you ever made things happen? Wished for something then...boom, it was there?"

"No!" she denied.

"Yes," Shane replied in the same instant.

She shot him a glare. "I think I'd know—"

"You did it at Purgatory. You didn't even realize it."

"No." He was wrong. Had to be.

But he nodded and said, "When we were together in that cave, you wished that I'd tell you what was going on. I did."

"But—"

"And you wished that we could make it out and that the seaplane would be there to take us to safety. It was."

She pointed at Pate. "Because he sent it there! Not because I did some mojo magic wishing!"

Pate cleared his throat. "I felt like something bad was happening. I went with my gut, against every protocol I've ever followed. It was almost as if I were...compelled to send Connor to Purgatory on that plane."

Her heart was beating too fast. Her palms were sweating, and her knees felt like jelly. Yet she still said, "You know what that is called? Coincidence! Not magic!"

"The blood work will be done soon," the woman murmured. "We'll have more than magic then."

She didn't want them analyzing her blood. *I don't want them to see...*

A voice seemed to whisper in her head. *Hide. Protect yourself. I won't let them destroy you...I'll stop them all.*

Goosebumps rose on her arms.

Shane was still holding her and the only warmth she felt came from the connection with his hands.

"I want to help you," the woman said as she came closer. The woman even offered Olivia a faint smile. "My name is Holly, and, believe it or not, I even can understand what you're going through right now."

"Really? You've been held prisoner by the people you thought were going to help you?" Her head inclined toward a watchful Pate. "That guy over there betrayed you?"

Pate's gaze dipped to Holly. Torment flashed across his face. His expression stunned her. So maybe her comment about betrayal hadn't been so far off the mark. Wow. Interesting.

Olivia's head had stopped throbbing. That was a good sign. Maybe her next escape attempt would go better.

"We want to protect you," Holly told her. "That's why Pate is keeping you in custody."

Olivia's laugh mocked that idea.

Shane cleared his throat. "Olivia, you need to know that after we left, there were some...incidents at Purgatory."

She didn't like that guarded note in Shane's voice. "You mean more than the hell that went down *before* we got out of there?" Things had gotten worse?

"Pate's men made it to the island. The prisoners...most of them are still secure."

She wet her too dry lips. "Most?"

Pate and Shane shared a hard look. *Definitely not good.* Shane released Olivia and eased back. She missed his touch because he'd taken that precious warmth away with him.

"The FBI agents can't find David Vincent."

Horror flooded through her, but Olivia managed to say, "He's hiding somewhere on the island. Probably — probably in some of the same places we used."

"They also can't find Case Killian." Pate's expression was grim as he delivered this news. "His guards reported that the warden was attacked by David, bitten — "

"So he's dead?" Olivia whispered.

"Dead…or he transformed. But either way, we don't know where he is." Pate's lips thinned. "And if anyone else at Purgatory knew a way off the island, it would be him. The warden had an all-access pass to the place."

Okay, now she was scared. Terrified. "I-it's not like Case would come after me."

They all stared at her.

"There's a bigger picture at play here," Pate explained quietly. "You're part of that picture. Maybe you didn't know what you were before you went into that prison, but someone else did. That someone sent you to Purgatory so that you could be used. Used by David…because he was one of the prisoners I was told you *must* see…or used by Case because he was the warden running the show there. Either way, someone wanted your power."

Shane thrust back his shoulders. "They aren't getting her."

Her gaze darted from face to face. Holly had edged closer to the silent, blue-eyed man. A man who watched the byplay with a dangerous intensity. Pate had closed in on Olivia, and Shane — Shane was watching her with a tight, worried expression.

Oh, hell. They were all dead serious. They thought that Case and David might actually come after her. "What happens if Case gets me? If David does?" She'd been so furious to find herself Shane's prisoner that she hadn't realized...*something much worse could be waiting out there for me.*

"They use you," Pate said flatly. "Just like I know how to cage you, there are others out there who know exactly how to set your power free."

"I have no power!"

Pate glanced at Holly. "How much longer until that blood analysis is done?"

"Just a few hours."

He nodded. Pointed toward Olivia. "You stay here until that analysis is back." His gaze slid to Shane. "I'm guessing you're playing guard now?"

A slight inclination of Shane's head was his only response.

"Seeing as how you attacked her last guard," Pate murmured, "I thought that might be the case." He gave a little salute toward Shane. "Make sure she doesn't leave."

"She won't go anyplace without me."

Holly cast Olivia an apologetic glance, then she slipped from the room. Whoever the guy standing in the shadows had been—well, he hurried right after that woman.

Pate hesitated near the door. "I didn't...I didn't want you to be hurt, Dr. Maddox."

Join the club.

"You'll have to make a choice soon," he continued as he glanced back at her. "You can keep trying to deny the truth, denying what you are, or you can use your powers. You can help us in the war that's coming."

She hadn't signed up for a war.

"Others know about you. They won't let you just vanish. They won't let you go back to the normal life that you had."

Her old life seemed so very far away.

"You wanted to know about the monsters, well, guess what? Now you're one of us."

The door closed softly behind him.

Olivia stared at that closed door for a few lost seconds, then she turned her gaze toward Shane. He was watching her, his stare so deep and consuming.

And angry. So very angry.

When he stepped toward her, Olivia tensed.

That stiffness just seemed to make him even angrier.

"Shane—"

He was at her side. Just like that. "Don't ever do it again."

"Uh..."

He sat on the bed. Pulled her toward him. "Don't ever make me feel fear like that again."

He'd been afraid?

His fingers curled around her chin. Held her so carefully. "The motorcycle is totaled. You went flying. When I got to you..." He gave a grim shake of his head. "You weren't moving. I thought you were dead."

She hadn't realized that the wreck had been so bad. No wonder people kept asking about her healing ability.

Her lashes lowered. She couldn't keep looking him in the eyes then. There was no more room for denial, not when it was just the two of them. "The markings hold me in." *If* Pate had been telling the truth, then there was only one reason those red markings would hold her captive.

"Yes."

"You think...you think I'm a djinn?"

He used his light hold on her chin to tip her head up so that she had to look into his eyes. "I know you're not human. I know you taste like no one else, and when I have your blood..." He was so close to her. "There's power in it. Power greater than a werewolf's, and I've known vamps who grew addicted to the rush from a shifter's blood...*because their blood is supposed to be that damn good.*" His fingers tightened a bit around her chin. "But yours is better. A hundred fucking times better. You aren't human, love, I knew that from the first taste."

He was telling her the truth. The terrifying truth. "You're keeping me here…to protect me?"

"There are people out there who will use you. I don't know what kind of powers you possess, but you were sent to Purgatory for a reason."

Pate had implied—no, basically *said* – that a war was coming. And she'd be an instrument in that war. "I don't want to hurt anyone."

His lips brushed against hers. A hot surge seemed to roll through her whole body at that sensual caress. "You won't."

Don't make promises that you can't keep. Or that I can't.

Her fingers lifted and curled around his shoulders.

"Don't make me fear again," he whispered those words against her lips. "When you do, I lose control."

He kissed her again. This time, his tongue slid past her lips. Swept inside. She kissed him back, her heart beating faster and faster as she savored him.

Desire rose within her. Wrong time, wrong place but… "Why didn't you feed?"

His muscles hardened beneath her touch.

"You could have taken from someone else, but you didn't." Very *un*vampire like. "Why?"

He kissed her again. "Something has changed." He pulled back a bit, stared into her eyes. "*You* changed me."

The words sounded like a warning. "I didn't mean to."

"No other will do for me."

She could only shake her head—and still taste him on her lips.

"I wasn't bitten, Olivia. I was never a human who was transformed into a vampire. I was never a human at all."

His fingers slid down her throat. Rested right over her racing pulse point. "You healed from the crash, but my bite still marks you." His eyes narrowed on her face. "Because you're mine. The mark is proof of that."

She was in so far over her head. Olivia fought to make sense of the madness and the magic. "Vampires are created from a virus." There was a big, scientific explanation for them. At least, that was what her research had shown her. The files that the Para Unit had allowed her to see. The bite spread the virus, and it mutated in its host and—

"I told you, love, I was never human."

She could see the edge of his fangs.

"My lineage is ancient. Unending. We don't follow the rules that constrain other vampires."

Sunlight hadn't weakened him. "Ancient," she whispered back. "Just how ancient are we talking here?"

"The Vikings thought we were gods."

Okay, definitely much older than she'd thought.

"I don't need as much blood to survive as other vampires do. Sunlight can never hurt me, but I do have a weakness. One."

His stare seemed to pierce straight through to her soul. "What's that?" Like he was going to tell her.

"You."

***

"Is it really a good idea to leave them alone together?" Connor asked as he glanced at the cabin's closed door.

Eric Pate shrugged. "It's the best idea we've got. You saw the way he was with her. There's no way Shane will let that woman out of his sight."

Connor rubbed his jaw. "Yeah, I saw the way he went for my throat and that shit wasn't normal."

Holly and Duncan had gone back to her lab, another cabin located within the shelter of the trees.

"She's doing something to him," Connor continued, voice rasping. "Twisting him up somehow."

Yes, Eric was afraid that was happening. But maybe he could use the changes. Maybe he could make them work… "I need you to take perimeter duty. If anyone comes this way, you'll smell them long before we see them." Because Connor was an alpha werewolf. Powerful, with senses far better than any human could ever dream. "We can't let anyone else get Dr. Maddox." And he knew that was exactly what would happen. She'd be tracked. Taken. Used.

Shane won't let that happen. Or at least, the vamp had better not.

"You really think the werewolves are coming?" Now Connor sounded as if he were looking forward to the fight. Wolves and their bloodlust. They were almost as bad as vamps.

"Yes." And he thought the mastermind of this twisted plot was coming, too.

Senator Donald Quick.

He'd been suspicious of that smug bastard for too long. The guy had been so determined to cage the dangerous paranormals, ignoring all of Pate's arguments.

Quick had been the one to first push the FBI to set up a Para Unit. The senator had seemed so good, on paper.

But when Eric had met the fellow in person…

I didn't trust him.

Connor turned away, but before he could leave, Eric grabbed his shoulder. "You and Duncan…you going to be okay working so closely with him?"

Connor's laugh held a bitter edge. "Are you trying to see if I still want to kill my brother?"

Yes, he was. The two men were brothers—brothers with one very vicious past.

"Relax," Connor told him. "Right now, the only guy scheduled for payback from me…that's Shane. The vamp is gonna get an ass-kicking when this mess is clear."

But Connor hadn't looked at Eric when he gave that little speech. Eric knew Connor was still tangled up on the inside.

Once upon a time, a time not so long ago, Eric and his agents had hunted Connor. They'd sent him to Purgatory.

And Eric had realized how very easy it was to mistake the good guys for the bad. Especially when there really wasn't a difference between them.

"Make sure you don't go after your brother again because Holly would be angry." And Holly was *his* family. Eric's only family. A step-sister who meant more to him than anything else. "Then I'd have to kill you."

Connor shook his head, as if he were trying to decide if Eric were serious or not. He was dead serious. When it came to Holly, he always was.

When he was sure his message had been received, Eric let go of the werewolf.

Then he stalked after Holly. He needed that blood work, ASAP.

He also had to figure out a permanent solution for the Olivia Maddox problem. Because there was no way he could let a djinn run loose on his watch. No damn way.

***

"Certain individuals are..." Shane's laugh was rough. Hell, explaining this wasn't going to be easy. Especially since he pretty much just wanted to growl out *You're mine*. Only that wouldn't be civilized.

He'd lived through plenty of uncivilized times.

He'd also already scared Olivia enough.

He could keep himself in check. Mostly.

"Certain individuals," he tried again, "make better...mates for vampires."

Her lips were red from his mouth. Moist. He wanted to take those lips again. Wanted to sample the blood that rushed through her veins.

"Did you just say 'mate'?"

He nodded. "I'm sure Holly could explain it with her biology. Science can explain away nearly all the magic these days." *Nearly.* Thanks to science, vampirism was some sort of virus that humans caught. Werewolves could be harnessed and controlled with silver collars. Once, though, things had been different. Villagers had run from the monsters that stalked their nights. They'd run from him.

He ran his tongue over the edge of his fangs. Whenever Olivia was near, his fangs sharpened, as if preparing for a bite. And he sure could use a bite now.

Would she come for him again? Shudder and moan with pleasure when his fangs pierced her?

"I told you…" Shane murmured. "I was born this way. That means any children I have…they'd be like me."

Her eyes were so wide. And deep.

"I aged normally until my thirtieth year, until my body was in peak condition, then time seemed to stop for me."

"Shane—"

"Only certain women can mate with me. Women like you. Women of power who are very, very rare."

She shook her head.

"My kind has fought for mates. We've slaughtered, battled, because we know how valuable you are."

"I'm not your mate."

She could be.

"I don't want another." A fucking telling sign for him. "The thought of drinking from another woman repels me. Your blood is in me, and it makes me need you. Makes me need more." His fingers were still at her throat. "It makes me want to take everything you have to give."

Her pulse raced beneath his touch.

"You like the bite, Olivia. You *love* it. You were meant to be with a vampire. A perfect mate." As he'd thought before…a vampire's wet dream. "That's why you always had the fascination with monsters. Because you were drawn in, something inside of you recognized what you wanted—"

"Stop." Her voice was low, shaking. "I'm some kind of genie, you're a Viking vampire, and now I'm supposed to mate with you?"

Actually, he'd been around since before the Vikings. And she was the first female that he'd felt the bond with.

He'd been warned before...

You'll drink from her and want no other.

His father's words. Of course, he'd had to kill that ruthless bastard on a battlefield one thunderous night. The bloodlust had been too strong within his father. He'd gone on another rampage.

So many bodies. Men. Women. Children.

Shane had stopped his father, once and for all. He'd taken his head, right after his father begged for mercy.

You never showed your prey any mercy. Those had been Shane's final words to the man who was far more devil than vampire.

Shane tried to shove that memory away. The past didn't matter. Olivia mattered. She was his present. His future. Everything that he needed.

"You're wrong." Her voice was soft, but he heard her perfectly. "You're so wrong about me. The reason I studied the monsters wasn't because I was drawn to them. It was because —"

When she stopped, he just waited.

"Because there's darkness in me." Whispered. Such a quiet confession. "I can feel it sometimes, pushing to get out. The darkness is there, in half forgotten dreams that haunt me. In nightmares that seem too real. In —"

A werewolf's howl split the night. Shane surged to his feet because he knew that howl belonged to Connor — and the guy was sending up a warning signal.

He headed for the door.

"Wait!"

Shane glanced back. Olivia had jumped from the bed. She had the sheet wrapped around her because after the wreck, they'd needed to cut her clothes away.

"What's happening?"

There was only one reason Connor would send up an alarm like that. "Company."

"And you're *leaving* me here? No, you can't do that." She motioned to the floor. "Get rid of the marks. Let me out! Let me come with you!"

But she'd tried to run from him before.

The howl came again, and…he could hear growls drifting on the wind. More than one beast was hunting in the darkness.

"I'm not leaving you," Shane told her. As if he would. They were past that now. She had far too much value to him. "I'm making damn sure no one gets to you."

Then he yanked open that door and rushed out to face the beasts who mistakenly thought they'd take her from him.

***

Olivia's jaw dropped. One minute, Shane had been telling her that he was her mate or some other fated nonsense, and in the next instant, he'd left.

While she was basically stuck there, naked.

Hell, no.

Olivia started searching the cabin, or as much of it as she could. Howls and snarls were sounding in the distance, and goosebumps pretty much covered her skin.

Clothing was her priority. She couldn't face whatever threat was out there while she was bare-assed naked.

There!

A bag was on the floor. She opened it, and found a t-shirt and jeans inside. Her size. Yes! Maybe the clothes had come from Pate. He struck her as the resourceful type. Right then, she didn't care who'd brought them. Olivia was just glad they were there. She jerked on the tennis shoes that were in the bottom of the bag and stood up.

That was when the silence hit her. No more growls. No more howls. Nothing.

Olivia crept toward the door, or rather, as far toward it as her invisible cell would allow. "Shane?"

No answer.

She bit her lip. She wanted to scream for him, but a scream would just give away her location. *Right, like the werewolves can't smell you!*

Her nose twitched then, because she'd just smelled something. Something that smelled a whole lot like...*fire.*

She whirled around. Saw the flash of flames right outside of the cabin's window. That flash grew, grew...and suddenly, fire was eating up the side of the cabin and rushing toward the ceiling.

She opened her mouth and screamed as loud as she could. *"Shane! Shane, I —"*

A werewolf leapt through the fire and came straight at her.

CHAPTER NINE

Shane shoved back the werewolf who'd just gone for his throat. He heard bones crunch when the wolf hit the ground, but he didn't care.

Ambush.

They weren't just facing off against one or two wolves. Not just that bastard David or the warden…a whole pack had attacked them. A pack that had closed in quickly — a pack that wasn't stopping.

Connor was in werewolf form. Fighting fiercely. Biting. Clawing.

Duncan was near his brother. Slashing with his own claws and protecting Connor's back.

Holly was outside. Firing silver bullets at the beasts and Pate —

"Fire!" Pate roared.

Hell, yeah, Shane knew about the fire. He could smell it, too. The pack had come in from the east, and they'd torched the med cabin first. Duncan had gotten Holly out of that place with a bellow of fury.

The wolves who'd been foolish enough to try and hurt Holly were dead on the ground.

"Shane!"

Olivia's scream reached him over the fury of the flames. He whirled and saw the fire shooting up from *her* cabin. *No!*

Two wolves tried to take him down.

They were the ones to fall, and they didn't get back up.

He kicked in the door of the cabin. "Olivia!"

She was on the floor, backing away from two wolves who stalked toward her. One was a big, hulking white wolf. A wolf with bright eyes that were fixed solely on Olivia. The other beast was a heavy, muscled gray wolf with bright, blue eyes.

The white wolf was familiar to Shane. He'd seen that beast on Purgatory. That beast had been *hunting* them both there.

David. The bastard had tracked Olivia to the mainland.

And the fire was spreading around the cabin. Too fast.

"Get away from her!" Shane lunged for them.

The white wolf sprang away from Olivia and came at Shane with his fangs snapping. Shane caught the beast's mouth, slammed its jaws shut and then threw the wolf right toward the flames.

The white wolf—David—howled in agony, and rolled, trying to put out the flames that spread on his fur.

"Stop!" Olivia's cry. "Stay back!"

Shane whirled. She had a broken chair leg in her hand and she was shoving it against the gray wolf. But the beast wasn't stopping.

Above Shane, the ceiling gave a low, long groan. He looked up and saw the flames rolling overhead. Shane knew the ceiling was going to collapse. Shit, Pate had said something about djinn and fire. *Blood and fire?*

He used his strength and raced toward Olivia. He caught her, shoved her back, but a force field seemed to rip her right out of his hands.

The markings on the floor… the fucking bottle cage that Pate had set! It was still trapping her. "Olivia!"

She was on her hands and knees.

He shoved away the markings, smearing them in a frantic fury.

The gray wolf locked its mouth around her leg and hauled her back toward him, just as the ceiling gave way and fire rushed down on them.

"Olivia!"

***

Eric Pate heard the guttural cry and he leapt into the flames. He *hated* fire. Such a pain in his ass.

Shane was burning. Flames were on the vamp's clothes. Rippling along his skin, and the fool was trying to go *deeper* into the fire.

Eric grabbed him and tried to drag the guy out of the cabin.

Fire could kill a vamp. Damn easy. Too—

Shane tossed him aside. When Eric crashed onto the floor, he was pretty sure that he broke his left wrist and dislocated his shoulder. He coughed as the smoke thickened around him. He was near the cabin's door. Shane had almost thrown him through that door.

But then *he* was being jerked to his feet. Duncan McGuire was in front of him, and the flames were everywhere.

"Pate, are you all right?" Duncan demanded.

Eric fumbled for his weapon. He hated to do this, but there wasn't a choice for him. "We have to…get Shane out." There were only a few people he considered to be his friends in this world. Shane was one of those precious few.

He and Duncan headed into the thick of the fire. Shane was clawing at part of the ceiling — the ceiling that had fallen down on the bed and now covered half of the floor.

The vampire was so frantic. Eric knew there was only one reason he'd react that way.

Olivia was under that collapsed, burning ceiling.

The fire was blazing in hot, angry bursts, and the flames were eating everything in their path. If they didn't get the vamp out, in the next five seconds, Shane would be dead.

Duncan grabbed Shane. The vamp whirled, snarling, "I have to get her, I have to get—"

Eric shot Shane. A wooden bullet straight to the heart. A guaranteed way to stop a vamp in his tracks. Shane's body shuddered as he collapsed, and Duncan dragged the vamp out of there.

They all barely made it outside before the cabin seemed to implode. Fire shot toward the sky in big, wild streaks of orange and gold.

Duncan dropped Shane to the ground. The vamp wasn't moving. Stiff, hard — dead. For the moment. He'd stay that way until Eric dug the wooden bullet out of the guy's heart.

Eric turned his head and saw that a big, white wolf was pacing a few feet away. The other wolves had assembled behind the beast. They weren't attacking, not yet.

What are they waiting for?

Then Connor jumped in front of Eric. Connor was bloody, battered, and in human form, but claws sprouted from his fingertips. "Who wants to try and go through me?"

The white wolf snarled.

Then the wolf whirled and ran into the woods. All of the other shifted werewolves followed him. They left their dead behind.

The cabin kept burning.

Connor rushed forward, as if he'd go after them.

"No!" Eric shouted. "That's what they want." He shook his head. "It's a set-up. Hell, it always has been." No one should have been able to access this safe house. No one.

I thought the traitor was in the FBI. Because that had been the Intel he'd received. Intel that hadn't revealed the full truth about the traitor. *I didn't realize he was the one running the whole damn show.* He'd made the connection with Senator Quick too late. With his resources, the senator would be able to discover all of the secrets that the Para Unit possessed.

"We need to get out of here." Eric ignored his throbbing wrist and shoulder. "Now."

Because those wolves weren't done.

Neither am I.

Holly's soft gasp reached him and he turned to see her falling to her knees beside Shane. Burns covered Shane's arms and chest. The side of his face was lined with blisters. The burns wouldn't heal until the bullet was out of him.

Holly cast a glare at Eric. "Do you always have to shoot us?"

Because he'd once put a wooden bullet in his sister, too. *I didn't have a choice.* Jaw locking, he glanced away from her. "I saved his life."

Connor paced back to him. "Where's Dr. Maddox?"

Black smoke drifted in the air above the flames.

"Aw, fuck," Connor muttered. "He'll go insane."

"That's why you didn't need to hunt the werewolves." He looked back down at his old friend. Holly was digging the bullet out of Shane's chest. "He'll destroy them all." Because Eric had realized what was happening between Shane and Olivia Maddox.

Something that *could* have been great.

Something that had been dangerous.

Something that was…gone.

"Almost got it," Holly whispered. "Almost…"

The wind seemed to moan around them. A sound of pain. Suffering.

The black smoke thickened above the fire.

"Got it!"

He looked at her hands. Saw the blood-stained fingers, the small, wooden bullet and—

Shane sucked in a deep gulp of breath. His eyes flew open. The burns on his face began to heal as he yelled, "Olivia!" Shane tried to leap to his feet, but Duncan and Eric held him down. The last thing they needed was for him to burn again, especially since they'd just saved his life.

But there was no holding Shane, not for long. With a strength that Eric hadn't seen before, Shane broke free of their grip. He staggered to his feet. Stared at the fire. Eric knew exactly what the vamp was planning.

"I will shoot you again," Eric swore. "You're not going back into those flames. You know the fire will kill you."

"Olivia!" Her name was a tormented cry.

And the fool started to run to the fire. Hell, *another* bullet to the heart? Was that what it would take? Was he going to have to shoot his friend again?

But then the flames just...died away. In an instant, the crackling of the fire stopped. Smoke drifted lightly in the air.

"I can...smell her," Duncan said, sounding stunned.

Connor faced the charred remains of the cabin. "So can I." He sounded just as stunned as Duncan. "She should be dead, just ash, but I can smell her."

Oh, hell.

According to the FBI files that he'd accessed, the way to kill a djinn was supposed to be a deadly combination of fire and blood. But the way to wake up a djinn's powers...the way to summon the darkness within...

Black smoke snaked toward them as they all stood there, frozen.

The smoke slowly dissipated.

And when the smoke vanished, Olivia was there. Her clothing had burned away, but her flesh appeared unmarred. She walked straight toward them with slow, certain steps.

"Olivia?" Shane ran toward her. His hand locked around her arm, and as soon as he touched her, a rush of black smoke swirled in the air again.

The djinn are creatures of smoke and magic. He'd read that notation in the files he'd accessed.

Olivia collapsed in Shane's arms. He lifted her up, held her closely against his chest. His eyes were wild, his expression maddened as he whirled toward Eric. "A werewolf bit her," Shane said, voice ragged. "Right before the fire...I saw him bite her! She needs help! *Help!*"

Holly scrambled to his side, but Eric didn't move.

He knew Olivia Maddox was beyond help.

***

She hurt…a damn lot.

Olivia groaned and opened her eyes. She was in a strange bed. An unfamiliar room. And she was handcuffed.

Was this becoming the story of her life?

She tugged on the cuff. It was linked to the side of what looked like a hospital bed.

A door creaked open. Footsteps padded toward her. Olivia glanced over and saw Holly pause near the bed. "You tried to attack me the last time I was here," Holly said softly. "The handcuffs were for my protection." A brief pause. "If you're back in control, I can take them off."

"I'm in control." Her voice sounded funny to her own ears. Too husky and raspy. Olivia cleared her throat.

Holly unhooked the cuffs.

Olivia thought about springing toward the woman, but she had promised not to hurt her. For the moment, anyway.

"Where am I?" Olivia asked and her voice still sounded funny. Like someone else was talking.

"We brought you in to one of the Para Unit's containment areas. Pate thinks you will be safer here because it's a place that isn't…on the books. The only people who know about it are those of us here now."

Olivia licked her lips and swore she tasted ash. "The fire — is Shane all right?" She remembered seeing him, right before that burning ceiling had come crashing down onto her.

"He's fine. Relax." Holly backed up a few steps. "You're the one who was…injured."

Olivia glanced down at her body. She didn't see any wounds.

"A werewolf bit you."

Olivia flinched. She didn't remember that part. At all.

"So, according to all the information I know, a werewolf bite means that you should be dead or transforming." Holly shook her head. "But that's not happening. Not with you."

Olivia's breath whooshed out. Holly was wrong. Or she was lying. "I-I wasn't bitten."

"You may just be the cure for the werewolf infection. A person who isn't susceptible, who has a natural immunity against the bite."

No. *There is no cure for a werewolf bite.* Olivia swung her legs to the side of the bed. Stood up. Her knees didn't even wobble, awesome. *Where is Shane?* She felt a hard urgency within her, a need to find him. Right then.

"I finished your blood work."

There was a note of hesitation, almost fear, in Holly's voice. Olivia crept toward her.

"I finished right before the werewolves attacked." Holly tilted her head to the side. "You aren't human, not fully."

Olivia stiffened her spine.

"But I think you knew that, right? I think you have been holding out on us all, Dr. Maddox."

Olivia glanced toward the door. "Is Shane outside?"

"Shane was willing to burn to protect you."

That news rocked through Olivia.

"But you walked away from the fire without a scratch. You stand there right now, no expression on your face, when I've just told you that you aren't human."

She might not be showing her emotions but it sure felt as if Olivia were shattering on the inside.

"Which side are you on?" Holly asked her.

Olivia shook her head. "I don't know what you mean."

Anger tightened Holly's delicate features. "Yes, you do."

She marched toward the door, but Holly leapt in her path and bared her fangs at Olivia.

The woman was a vampire?

"It's not as simple as a choice between good and evil," Holly said. "Because maybe we've all got evil in us. All got some good too. It's a choice about survival. Are you going to join the supernaturals out there when they attack the humans? When they stop hiding and come out full force? Or will you try to protect the innocents before they get slaughtered?"

She'd always wanted to help people. Always wanted to stop the monsters. "I wish I could stop them all," Olivia said softly. If only. "But I can't."

Holly opened her mouth to speak, but smoke blew from her lips. Black smoke. Holly grabbed her throat as she fell to the floor.

"Holly!" Horror tore through Olivia as she grabbed for the other woman. Holly was convulsing on the floor. Smoke rising from her body. "She needs help!" Olivia cried even as her fingers flew over Holly's body in an attempt to find out what was happening. "Help—"

The door flew open. Shane and Pate rushed inside. Pate immediately fell to his knees beside Holly. His gaze flew over her, assessing, then he grabbed Olivia in a grip that hurt. "What did you do?"

She shook her head. "Nothing—"

"Pate, get your fucking hands off her," Shane warned.

Holly gasped, struggling to breathe.

"What did you do?"

"I-I said I wished I could stop them!" Those had been the last words she'd spoken before Holly collapsed on the floor.

Pate's eyes widened. "Un-fucking-wish that." He shook her. "Un—"

Shane yanked him back.

Holly's skin was ghostly pale. "I take it back," Olivia whispered. Had she truly done this?

"Rescind it!" Pate barked. "Say you rescind the damn wish!"

"I-I rescind the wish."

Holly sucked in a deep gulp of air. The smoke stopped rising from her skin. Light color slowly filled her cheeks.

Olivia's shoulders slumped.

"Told you..." Holly gasped out as her fingers caught Pate's. "She'd...do the right thing."

Olivia's gaze jumped between Holly and Pate. Then to Shane. Only...Shane wasn't looking her in the eyes.

She slid back as Pate helped Holly rise to her feet.

"It was too risky," Pate snapped back to Holly. "And the plan was for her to focus that power on me, not you."

Olivia's hand flew out and she steadied herself on the bed. "You set me up?"

Holly took a few more, deep breaths.

Shane still hadn't moved. What was up with that?

"A test," Pate explained. "After the way you, um, rather impressively walked through fire before, we realized that your dormant powers must have been activated." His hand rubbed Holly's shoulder. "Blood and fire...guess they can kill djinns and bring them to life."

Her stomach was in knots. "I thought I was hurting her!"

"You were," Holly said with a quick wince. "Burning me alive." She glanced at Pate. "The part about the djinn's wishes being twisted up is true, too. She said she wished she could stop all the monsters, and the next thing I know, I'm tasting fire."

"Yeah..." Pate drawled out the word as he focused on Olivia. "How about you do us all a big favor and don't make *any* wishes for a while? At least not until we can learn more about just what you can and can't do."

Her hands wrapped around her stomach. They'd just experimented on her. She'd thought—Olivia shook her head and focused on Shane. "Why did you let them do this to me?"

A muscle flexed along the hard line of his jaw.

"Why?"

He didn't answer her. Rage pumped through Olivia. "Dammit, I wish—"

Shane was in front of her in an instant, and his hand was over her mouth. "No more wishes." His voice was low, gruff. "No more."

"Ah...I think we should give them some privacy," Holly murmured.

Olivia didn't look away from Shane.

"Don't kill him," Pate called as he turned to leave. "We need him alive." Then the door closed behind him and Holly with a squeak.

Shane's hand was still over her mouth. His eyes glinting at her. Betrayal burned within Olivia. She'd thought he was on her side, but—

She yanked away from him. "Don't touch me."

His hands fisted at his sides. "That's not really an option for me."

She noticed his pallor then. He was almost as pale as Holly had been moments before. And his eyes...dark shadows surrounded his eyes and the faint lines on his face seemed deeper.

"Just to warn you, my control is razor fucking thin."

A shiver slid over her. Hell, was it any wonder she was shivering? She was dressed in a paper-thin hospital gown. Olivia saw a bag near the door. She opened it. Found jeans, a shirt, shoes—all the clothing she'd need inside. Turning her back on Shane, she changed as quickly as she could, but she felt his stare on her. Every second.

"I thought you died," he said when she turned back to face him. "I thought I *let* you die. The flames were everywhere, and I couldn't get to you."

Her breath slid out in a fast rush. Some of her fury eased because she could feel his pain in the room around them.

"Something broke then."

She didn't understand.

"In me…" And he stalked toward her. "I think the darkness got out. Pate should have seen it, but he didn't." He caught her wrist. Lifted it to his mouth. Pressed a hot kiss to her racing pulse. *The darkness got out.*

His teeth sank into her wrist.

She tried to pull away from him, even as pleasure pulsed through her body. Pleasure that came in long, drugging waves.

He was drinking from her. Licking her skin with his tongue. Pulling her against the hot, hard cradle of his body.

Desire, lust, built within her. She should have shoved him away. Instead, Olivia rubbed against him as the pleasure surged and surged and her climax—

"No!" Olivia ripped her wrist from him and stumbled away from Shane.

His lips were dark—her blood was on his lips. His fangs were out. His eyes blazed with a wild passion.

"You're trying to control me." Her heartbeat wouldn't slow. "Another test, just like what they did." She couldn't trust him. Couldn't trust anyone.

But Shane shook his head. "This is no test." His eyes were filled with a dark tangle of emotions. Need. Anger. A hard edge of possession. "I need you…to survive."

Okay, now that scared the crap out of her. "I want to leave this room. I want you to move out of my way." Her wrist was throbbing, but it wasn't a painful throb. Pleasure seemed to vibrate through her in time with each little pulse.

Shane inclined his head, and he backed away. She hurried past him and pulled open the door. Olivia wasn't quite sure what she expected to find outside of that room—maybe another prison-like facility, but the bright lights and gleaming floor just appeared strangely…normal.

She hurried down the hallway, far too conscious of Shane's footsteps behind her. She passed offices. Saw desks, phones. But no people.

She stilled in the middle of that hallway and turned to face Shane. "Where is everyone?"

His face was tense. "This facility hasn't been used in a while. It's a back-up location." He hesitated, then said, "It's a place that the senator doesn't know about. It wasn't officially on the Para Unit's books."

"Stop it," she whispered as she stared into his eyes and took a step away from him.

He advanced toward her. "Stop what?"

"Staring at me as if—"

"As if I want to eat you alive?" Another slow, gliding step. "But that's exactly what I want to do."

Her wrist throbbed again, and the pleasure seemed to roll right through her whole body. It shouldn't happen. She shouldn't be so attuned to him.

He'd said they could be mates. She didn't want his words to be true, did she?

"You realize that the senator was the one setting you up. Pulling the strings."

She shook her head. "Donald has been my friend for years." Her mother had worked as one of his aides. Donald's daughter had been her best friend when she was a kid. But that had been before...

Before Chloe changed.

She cleared her throat and retreated another step. "Donald pulled some strings to get me clearance for projects like this one, yes, but he wasn't using me. He was helping me." Shane and the others had it all wrong.

Shane shook his head. "Pate has known for some time that a powerful werewolf was setting a plan like this in motion. A plan that would turn humans into prey."

She turned away from him. Kept hurrying down that hallway. There had to be a way out of there. "You're wrong," she said again. "He's no werewolf." And this place was a maze. Her steps tapped faster against that gleaming tile.

In a blink, Shane was in front of her. She stopped, gasping. She hated that too-fast way he could move. Hated it.

"No, love, *you're* wrong, but I guess you'll have to figure that out for yourself, won't you?" He seemed sad then, but he pointed to the left. "You can leave that way. You'll even find a car waiting outside for you. Use the GPS navigation system, and you can be back home by nightfall."

No way. He was just going to let her go? "Are you serious?"

He nodded. "But it's a fucking ridiculous plan. The werewolves have your scent. You leave here, and they *will* find you."

"And the alternative is...what? To stay hidden here, a prisoner?"

"You wouldn't be a prisoner."

She would be. "For how long?"

"Until the threat is over."

That was pretty much not an answer. "And what happens if Pate gets the urge to bottle me up again?" She glanced to the right and saw the video camera perched on the wall there. No doubt, Pate was watching and listening to them at that very moment.

"I won't let him."

She wanted to trust him, but the door to the left was so close...Olivia slid away from him.

"Don't do this." His voice was flat. "It's going to be the wrong choice."

Her body felt cold. Her wrist—she pushed it against her side. "The werewolves won't find me. I can disappear." On *her* terms. Not Pate's.

"You don't want to stand with the Para Unit to face whatever the hell is coming?"

"I just want my life back." That door was temptingly close. "That's all."

Her hand pushed against the door.

"And what about me?"

The question sank into her, and, without looking at him, she found she could be honest in these last moments. "You scare me, Shane. You make me want things that I shouldn't. You make me...want you." She shoved against the door. Sunlight spilled inside and on her. "And the way I feel when I want you—" Wild, desperate, on the edge of control. "That terrifies me most of all."

She walked into the light and left him in the shadows.

***

The door clanged shut behind Olivia.

"You're really going to let her walk away?" Connor asked.

Shane had known the damn werewolf was close by. "Her life. Her choice."

You make me want things I shouldn't. You make me...want you.

Her blood had given him a rush, one that still had him feeling drunk—and needing more. "She doesn't want to be with the Para Unit." Not that he blamed her. They'd nearly killed her. He glanced at Connor, gave him a faint nod. "I can count on you for back-up?"

"Yeah, but you and Pate really need to work on coming up with better plans in the future. This one is shit." Connor leveled his stare at Shane. "You're risking your life for her. A woman you just met days ago."

The werewolf didn't get it. "I've been on this earth for more than two thousand years."

Faint surprise widened Connor's eyes.

"I've seen countries rise and fall. Watched more death and pain than you can imagine." Those memories would never fade. "I didn't think there was any pleasure left for me here, then I looked up on a storm-tossed ferry, and I saw her." In that moment, so much had changed for him.

"It's...it's the blood bond that I heard Pate talking about, isn't it? I overheard him telling Holly that the blood was tying you to Olivia because the woman was some sort of genetic match for a vampire—"

"It's not the blood. I was addicted to Olivia before my first taste." He could hear the car cranking outside. *Time to go.* "Tell Pate that the debt is paid."

Olivia didn't want to stay with the Para Unit. She didn't trust them. Fine.

He yanked open the door. Olivia was starting to pull away.

Did she really think he'd let her face the danger alone? He leapt forward and came down a few feet in front of her car. She slammed on the brakes and the scent of burning rubber filled the air.

Then she honked at him.

His lips twitched.

Olivia rolled down the window. "Vampire, are you crazy?"

He took his time walking to the passenger side of her vehicle. He climbed in. Stretched out.

"Uh...what are you doing?" Olivia demanded. She pointed to the nondescript building behind him. "Your team is in there."

"And the woman I want is right here." He caught her hand, lifted it to his mouth. Pressed a kiss to her wrist. "I'm not letting you go off alone, not with the werewolves out there." And with the senator ready to close in...

Olivia might think the man was her friend, but Shane held no such illusions.

"Wait...are you saying...you're...choosing me?"

She seemed stunned. Had she seriously thought he wouldn't keep protecting her? Now that was rather insulting. "Maybe one day," he told her quietly, "you'll choose me, too."

Olivia blinked those dark, gorgeous eyes of hers, eyes that could take a man to his knees.

"I'd advise against going to your place," he said and pressed one more kiss to her wrist. She shivered. "They'll be waiting there. After all, the senator knows where you live. The werewolves won't even have to bother tracking you. They'll just be staking out the place."

She bit her lower lip. "Donald...has always been good to me."

Donald is a dead man walking. "My place," he told her. "We'll be safer there."

He could see the hesitation in her eyes, but after a few moments, she nodded and slowly pulled her hand from his grasp.

The car accelerated smoothly, and they left the Para Unit behind.

***

From his office, Eric Pate watched the black vehicle drive away. "The game is in motion."

Behind him, Holly sighed. "People's lives aren't part of a game. How many times do I have to tell you that?"

He turned toward her and decided to ignore her question. "You're dead certain about the results of Dr. Maddox's DNA analysis and her blood work?"

"Yes. I don't make mistakes." Now she sounded a bit disgruntled because he'd questioned her, but Holly rallied quickly. "One of her parents was human, I'd bet my life on it."

Olivia Maddox wasn't the first hybrid he'd come across. She wouldn't be the last, either. And with the others, their paranormal sides had often been dormant, needing a trigger to emerge.

Blood and fire.

"He triggered her," Eric said, certain now of the senator's intent. "If you want to wake a beast, what better place to do it than in Purgatory?"

"But what is he going to do with her now?"

His fingers tapped against his chin. "That's what Shane will find out for us."

Hiding Olivia within the Para Unit would have done no good. Other agents — humans — would have just gotten caught in the crossfire when the attack came. Senator Quick had too many powerful friends and far too much pull in the FBI.

Hiding her wasn't an option, but using her as bait…that certainly was.

Holly raised her brows. "I get that Shane felt like he owed you…but *why* was that? I mean, if he's some all-powerful vamp — "

"He's the strongest vampire I've ever met." And he'd come across more than his share.

"Then how did you convince Shane that the guy actually owed you?"

He remembered a battle on sand that burned, and blood that formed the only river around them.

Before Eric had joined the FBI, he'd been an Army Ranger, working in the Middle East. "I met him on my second tour," he said, voice soft. He didn't usually talk about his Ranger days, not with anyone, even Holly. "Detonations were going off all around me. Screams were filling the air. And I thought I was going to die."

Holly didn't speak.

"There was a school up ahead. So small, right in the middle of that freaking desert. I could hear the children crying out from inside."

She flinched.

And he kept remembering. "Shane went to help the children." He could still hear the explosion. "I don't even know how the hell he got there, or why he was there, but when the detonation went off, a detonation that should have killed those kids, that fucking insane vamp was right on top of it." Absorbing the blast.

Nearly getting torn apart.

"Fire can kill a vamp." And Shane had been willing to run into fire for Olivia. *Don't give her that much of yourself, man.* "I helped him." An exchange of blood in a place where he could feel the cold touch of death. "We both made it out of there." And Eric …he was mostly alive now because of that change.

Mostly.

"You're his friend."

He was. "Yes."

She walked toward him. Tipped back her head. The smile that crossed her face was sad. "What do you think your friend will do to you if Olivia Maddox dies?"

He already knew. Shane was protective of his allies, but his enemies…he showed them no mercy. "He'll kill me."

CHAPTER TEN

"This isn't what I expected," Olivia said as she walked into the lush apartment that overlooked the lights of Seattle. Night had just fallen, but the buildings all around them glowed with illumination.

Shane shut the door behind them. "Let me guess...were you picturing some kind of medieval castle, maybe a dungeon, some restraints?"

Her cheeks flushed.

"Been there, done that." He stalked toward her. Brushed his hand over her cheek. "Would be willing to do it again in a heartbeat for you."

She caught his hand. "I don't understand you."

His smile flashed, and it was a predatory grin. "That drives you crazy, doesn't it? Your whole deal is that you have to understand the monsters. But maybe you can't figure out what makes us all tick. Maybe there are some things you'll never know."

His body was so close to hers, and the sensual awareness that he sparked within her just wouldn't lessen no matter how many times she tried to calm herself down.

Riding with him in the car had been close to torture. He'd filled that small space. Dominated it. Every time he'd shifted even a tiny bit, she'd been hyper aware of him.

"I want to know about you." And she did. This man had left the FBI behind, and he'd come with her. He kept protecting her, looking out for her. No one had done that before. After she'd lost her mother at eighteen, Olivia had been on her own.

I don't feel like I'm alone anymore.

He rolled his shoulders, but didn't pull away from her. "What if you don't like what you learn?"

"You're the white knight, the guy who keeps rushing to the rescue." Not the monster she'd thought. "What's not to like there?"

He shook his head. "I've been feared, rightfully so, for centuries."

She tightened her hold on him. "You were born a vampire."

"Do you understand what that means? The bloodlust, the hunger—they were with me, always. I grew up thinking it was normal to track and hunt prey…prey that was human."

She didn't let go.

"My father thought it was great sport to hunt humans. Of course, it was more challenging to go after the werewolves. And they tasted better."

"Shane…"

"That's what my life was. Death and pain. I was a monster. I *am* a monster. There are sins on my soul that can never be erased, no matter what I do."

Atonement. "That's why you work for the FBI. You're trying to make up for what you've done."

Now he did pull away. He strode toward the window. Stared out at the night. "A part of me always knew…what I was doing, what I *was*…it was all wrong. But when someone calls you a fucking god, hell, the power rush you get is too strong to deny."

He put his hands on the glass window pane.

"We ruled the world then, until I looked around and saw it was a world full of death and pain. The children begged for mercy, the women fled, and the men were in agony."

She shook her head, trying to shove away the images that his words pushed into her mind.

"My father was the leader. The most powerful vampire in existence, and he didn't expect an attack to come from the one he trusted above all others." His laughter held a cold, bitter edge. "Maybe that's why I was able to take his head. He trusted me too much to expect a betrayal."

He'd killed his own father? She hurried forward.

He turned to her. "You're supposed to back away when a man makes a confession like that. When he tells you of the bloodlust and the death, you should be afraid."

She was. Her breath felt cold in her lungs. "You haven't hurt me." Not once.

"Not yet," he said, his jaw tightening. "My father wanted me to be just like him. There was a village that was trying to resist him, trying to fight back against us. They called us devils, and my father wanted to show them what hell was truly like." His eyes were cloudy with memories. "I saw the children there. Terrified. And I saw my bloody past…it had to stop." His lips thinned. "So I stopped it."

There was pain there, filling the air all around him.

Then he smiled, and it was a chilling sight as his fangs flashed. "I could tell you good things, you know. About how I've saved lives. Stopped killers. But the scales never really balance, and I've always known, deep inside, that my father was right."

"Shane…"

"I am just like him. I have the same darkness. It pushes me. It calls to me. It tempts me." He paused. His eyes narrowed. "Or it did, until something else tempted me more."

He tempted her. Danger, darkness, a vampire with a past so bloody and tortured. But he tempted her.

"My earliest memory," she heard herself whisper, "is of being trapped by blood and fire. The fire was closing in on me and the blood…it was on my hands. My feet. I was screaming, but there was no escape for me."

He didn't speak. It was his turn to listen.

"I always knew something bad had happened to me, but I never could break through and figure out just what it had been. When I asked my mother, when I'd tell her about the nightmares that would never stop, she'd just whisper—"

Olivia broke off because now her mother's whispers made a strange sense to her. And they left her chilled.

"She'd wish that I would have peace," she finished, voice breaking. "And that the darkness would leave me alone."

Only it never had. The darkness had been a living, breathing thing inside of her. Whispering sometimes, twisting insidiously within her. And she'd sought out killers, others who must feel that same darkness because she'd wanted to control herself.

Wanted to stop whatever it was that seemed to live in her heart.

Djinn?

Yes.

Her gaze fell to his throat. "I can't believe Pate just let me go. Isn't he worried about what I might do?" A few wrong words had sent Holly to the floor.

"I'm not worried," Shane said softly. "Because you're strong. Far stronger than you seem to realize."

His words brought her eyes right back up to his.

"I want you," he told her, the words stark and hard. "And I will always want you. I look at you, and I fucking feel complete. Like I found something I didn't even know I was missing."

She wanted his words to be true. Wanted the strange connection she felt with him to be real.

Because she hadn't felt that connection with anyone else.

"I won't let anyone hurt you. Any who comes after you — human, vamp, werewolf — they'll have to go through me first."

He sounded so fierce. Her vampire.

She leaned into him. Put her hands on his shoulders. Made her choice. "And anyone who comes after you will have to deal with me." Because she wanted to see where this would go. Their connection, their desire…where would it take them?

She didn't care about some fated nonsense. She cared about the way he made her feel.

For so long, she'd felt as if she were the secret freak in the room, even when she was with killers.

But with Shane, Olivia felt as if she were desired, wanted, more than anything else.

As if she mattered more than anything else.

"Don't bite me this time," Olivia told him. "I want to see what it's like, when it's just us."

He gave a jerky nod.

She pushed onto her tip-toes and rose against him. Her lips pressed to his mouth, and her tongue slid over the crevice between his lips. Slowly, she licked the line there, savoring him for a moment even as the blood heated within her veins.

His lips parted and her tongue slid inside. His hands settled along her hips, his long, strong fingers curved around her ass, and he pulled her against the aroused length of his cock.

"Just us," she whispered against his mouth.

Would it be as good this time? Without that strange blood link?

He kept kissing her, and the kiss became even deeper, so sensual that she trembled.

He lifted her into his arms. Carried her away from the window and down a narrow hallway. He took her into his bedroom. Stripped her. Lowered her onto the bed.

"Your clothes," Olivia gasped. "You're still dressed!"

He caught her legs and, gently, carefully, pulled her to the edge of the mattress. "I won't bite," he promised her, "but I will taste."

He leaned over her. His mouth pressed a kiss to her throat, right above her racing heartbeat. He licked her, sucked the skin, had her moaning, and then he moved down.

Down her neck. Down her collarbone. Kissing. Caressing.

His fingers slid over her breasts. Strummed her nipples. Had the desire coiling so tightly within her. Then his mouth replaced his fingers. He took her nipple into his mouth and sucked, he laved her flesh, he had her hips arching up against him and her breath panting out.

Desire rolled through her on a red-hot wave. She wanted his clothes gone. Wanted to feel every inch of him against her. In her.

But he was kissing her stomach now. Being so careful not to hurt her. Being too careful when she needed, wanted, him to be wild right then.

"Shane!"

He parted her legs. "I told you, I get to taste."

He bent at the edge of the bed and put his mouth on her. His lips feathered over her sensitive core, and his tongue stroked against her clit.

She cried out his name and squeezed her eyes shut as a powerful flood of sensation overwhelmed her. *Yes!*

She arched toward him.

His tongue thrust into her. His fingers stoked her. His lips savored and he was driving her insane.

Her hands grabbed for the covers. She fisted them. Her body was bow tight as the release waited just beyond her reach.

He licked her clit.

She erupted. No other word for it. The pleasure exploded through her and she shrieked his name. The waves of release racked her again and again, and her sex contracted, shuddering with the pleasure that was so intense it was on the verge of pain.

It wasn't fleeting. Wasn't some quick pop of release. The climax left her weak, gasping…and wanting more. Her eyes opened, and Olivia stared at Shane. He'd stood, and, as she watched, he jerked off his shirt. Tossed it across the room. He shoved down his pants and his heavily aroused cock sprang toward her.

The blood link hadn't been some kind of aphrodisiac this time. She simply wanted him.

Olivia could see the edge of his fangs when he came down toward her, and his mouth went right to her throat. He kissed her. "You taste fucking delicious."

He drove into her, thrusting his cock fully inside of her. She was slick and sensitive from her release, and a gasp escaped her at his complete penetration.

"Olivia?"

She wrapped her legs around him. Raked her nails down his back. "When do I…get to see…how you taste?"

He withdrew, plunged again.

The tension coiled within her once more. The pleasure mounted.

They rolled across the bed. Wrecked those covers. He pinned her beneath him, opened her wide, and thrust down at an angle that sent the heavy length of his cock sliding right over her clit.

He knew what she liked. What made her go wild.

What made her come, screaming his name.

His hands closed around her fists. She'd grabbed the covers in a death grip again. "Look at me," he said, his voice a guttural demand.

She couldn't look anywhere else. His gaze trapped hers.

She saw the pleasure take him. Watched as his release turned his eyes an even darker shade. His cheeks flushed, his teeth snapped as he ground them together, and he came, pumping deep inside of her.

It took a few moments before her breath stopped escaping in wild heaves. Her heart raced frantically against her chest. He still held her hands, and his eyes were on hers.

She hadn't needed the bite to go wild. She'd just needed…him.

"Even better…" His voice sent a shiver skating over her. "Since we aren't in some shit-forsaken cave this time."

His words were so unexpected that a little laugh tumbled out of her.

Surprise flashed over his face, and his eyes narrowed. "I like that."

"What?" Her lips quirked at him. "Shit-forsaken caves?"

He freed her right hand. His fingers brushed against her cheek. "I like the dimple that you have right here."

Her smile slipped a bit.

"And I like the sound of your laughter."

She hadn't exactly been laughing it up with the guy, not with all of their life-or-death drama. But this was different. This moment, the aftermath. So intimate. There were no shields between them. There was nothing at all. She didn't need to hide from him, didn't have to pretend to be something she wasn't.

Her other lovers had been human. She'd always felt on edge when she was with them. As if she had to watch herself. *As if I had to fit in.*

When she hadn't even realized that she was different.

"Did I prove it to you?"

She shook her head, not understanding.

He kissed her, tasted her slowly. "Did I…" Shane said against her lips. "Convince you that the desire is just as strong without my bite?"

She nodded. Her heartbeat still hadn't returned to a normal speed.

"Good." But there was a note in his voice that had Olivia tensing. A dangerous rumble. "Because if I don't sink my teeth into you soon, I'll go fucking insane."

She turned her head. Offered her neck. Asked for what she wanted, "Bite me."

His teeth sank into her.

The pleasure rose once more.

***

Midnight was at hand. The fucking witching hour. Shane stared out at the darkness. He could feel the hunters in the night. Practically sense them closing in. He'd told Olivia that the danger wasn't over. He'd tried to warn her.

There would be no more warnings.

Sheets rustled behind him. He turned back and saw her sitting up in bed. Her hair was tousled, her cheeks flushed, and his mark was on her neck.

I want to keep her with me…forever.

For a vampire, forever was a very, very long time.

He wanted to give her a choice, but if she didn't choose him, Shane wasn't sure what he would do.

I just found her. I'm not prepared to let her go.

So he figured the plan had to be simple—*I need to make her love me.*

Okay, maybe not so simple.

"You look like you lost your best friend." She wrapped her hands around her knees. Her hair was a dark curtain running down her back. "What's wrong?"

There would be no point in deception. "They're coming."

She stiffened. "They?"

"I can smell them." Werewolves. In his building. He was a bit surprised that they'd taken such a direct approach. He'd thought they might try for a sneak attack.

Olivia jumped from the bed, giving him one gorgeous flash of her body before she started to frantically yank on her clothing.

He had on a pair of jeans, and he didn't move. He wasn't feeling so frantic. More pissed, yes.

The wolves need to leave us alone.

One way or another, they would.

"We have to get out of here!" She did a little dance as she shimmied into her jeans. Then she ran toward him and grabbed his arm. "Come on!"

He didn't move. "We don't have to worry about any humans getting caught in the crossfire here."

Her brow furrowed. "There are five floors below us—"

"I own them all. No one else is here." They'd entered the parking garage and taken the elevator straight up to his apartment. So Olivia hadn't realized how alone they'd been.

We aren't alone now. The werewolves are closing in.

"We still have to leave, we can't be sitting ducks—"

"I have the advantage here. The wolves were able to attack us so well at the cabin because they had the woods for cover. All of the animal scents were already there. Here it's different. I control everything here."

Her fingers tightened around him. Suspicion flashed on her face, but vanished almost instantly. "Control is great. Staying alive is even better. Let's *go.*"

He inhaled. "Two werewolves are coming up the elevator now. A man and a woman."

"Why aren't we leaving?" Again, suspicion flashed across her face.

"I won't let them hurt you," he promised.

And he saw understanding sink in. She looked at the bed. At him. "You control everything here," Olivia repeated his words in a quiet, hurt voice. "I-I was never free of the Para Unit, was I?"

The car had been equipped with a tracking system. Just in case she'd tried to slip away without him. She wouldn't have been able to go far. The Para Unit would have been able to remotely disable the car.

"Bait." She said the word like a curse. "You didn't want to compromise the precious location of the Para Unit, so you tossed me out? To the wolves?"

She had it wrong. "No one will hurt you." He sure as hell hadn't tossed her anyplace.

Olivia ran from the room. He followed her, body tense. "Olivia—"

She was at the window, looking down. "It's too high for me to jump."

Hell, yes, five stories up was too high for her to jump.

Olivia spun around and rushed for the door. "Guess that means I have to run."

He beat her to the door. This was the moment that they had been waiting for. The leverage the team needed. "They're on the other side of that door."

Her eyes were stark. "What have you done?"

He pushed her back. Opened the door. Stared at the man and woman waiting there.

It was easy enough to recognize the warden. Case Killian looked like hell, though. Deep lines marred his face. Dark shadows swept under his eyes, and stubble covered his jaw.

Shane had never met the woman who stood just beside Case, but he'd seen pictures of Chloe Quick. She was petite, deceptively fragile, with bright blue eyes and black hair that skimmed her shoulders.

"I need to see Olivia," Chloe said softly. Then she added, "Please." Her voice broke on the plea.

Shane lifted a brow but before he could speak, Olivia was hauling him out of her way. "Chloe? What are you doing here?"

Chloe's lower lip trembled. "I'm so sorry…"

"Sorry? Why?"

Olivia was far too trusting. "Because, love," Shane told her, his words an angry growl, "your friend Chloe is the one who set you up."

CHAPTER ELEVEN

Apparently, she couldn't trust anyone.

Chloe, Shane, and the warden — *the warden!* — were all pacing around the apartment like caged beasts.

Olivia sat on the couch, her spine ram-rod straight, her hands between her knees, and she tried to figure out just what the hell was happening.

"You…aren't the bad guy?" Olivia blurted to Case.

He stopped his pacing. Winced. "No, I kind of fucking am. Especially after getting bitten."

"He needs a cure," Chloe said, rubbing her arms, still pacing. "Just like I do."

"There *is* no cure for a werewolf bite. You know that!" Her words flew out, but…they were wrong. Because Holly had told Olivia that *she* had survived the werewolf bite. That *she* might be the cure.

Chloe swung toward her. Anger and pain battled in her eyes. "If that's the case, then why didn't you turn? We were both bitten when we were teens, Olivia. *Both* of us."

No, she didn't remember that. Olivia shook her head.

"You went down first. That whole pack — they came for *you*. You were bleeding, and I tried to help you." Chloe lifted her hands. Claws had sprouted from her fingertips. "But they turned on me. They bit me, clawed and attacked, and then they left us…to die."

Only they hadn't died. "I don't remember the attack." Because when the first wolf had leapt at Olivia, he'd knocked her to the ground. Her head had slammed into the concrete and she'd passed out. When she'd woken, Chloe had been on the ground beside her, covered in blood.

"You had already healed when the EMTs arrived," Chloe whispered. "They didn't believe you'd ever been bitten, but I knew the truth."

Shane's hand settled on Olivia's shoulder. He was — what? Trying to comfort her? Now? She glanced back at him. He stood behind the couch, behind her, and his face was a dangerous mask. "You told your father about Olivia," he accused Chloe.

Olivia glanced back at her friend and saw Chloe's head sag forward. "Yes. After I changed…I-I was desperate to go back. To be human again. I hated what I was."

"Not like it's a fucking cake walk for me," Case snapped.

Chloe flinched. "I thought if my father could just get a sample of your blood, that maybe he could find out what made you different. I tried asking you directly, but you acted like you had no idea what I was talking about."

Because she hadn't known. And she remembered… "That's why you insisted I give blood with you that time…" Hell, she'd thought she was participating in some kind of blood drive back then — several freaking blood drives — but all along, they'd been studying her?

Shane's hand tightened on Olivia's shoulder. "After he got the results of her blood work, your father knew Olivia was special, didn't he?"

Was "special" a code word for djinn?

Miserably, Chloe nodded. "He knew she was different, but he didn't know what she was."

Olivia's gaze slid to Case. "Is that where you come in? Did the senator pay you to find out what I was? To throw me in with those werewolves at Purgatory?" Only the plan had backfired, and Case had been the one bitten.

Case shook his head. "I'm not working for Senator Quick."

Uh, oh…If he wasn't working for the senator —

Shane's hand slipped from her shoulder. "He's working for the Para Unit. Another undercover agent that Pate sent in, only I didn't learn about the guy until yesterday." His voice was an angry rumble. "Until then, I just thought he was some dick who needed taking down. A psychotic asshole who got off on hurting the inmates."

Case braced his legs apart and glared at Shane. "And I thought he was some dick vampire out to destroy Purgatory. I wasn't told he was an agent, either."

A snarl slipped from Shane.

Case held up his hands. "So my methods are…unorthodox. The bastards in there are killers. What did you want me to do? Bake 'em brownies? They deserved what they had coming to them."

"Not your call to make," Shane snapped.

Olivia's temples throbbed.

Case's lips thinned and he said, "Look, Pate knew there was still corruption at Purgatory. He wanted someone in with the prisoners…" He inclined his head toward Shane. "And he wanted someone keeping tabs on the guards. I found out that Evan Jurant was the one who sabotaged your collar remote and he—"

She jumped to her feet. *Evan.* "He was the one who left me with the werewolves."

Case gave a grim nod. "If it makes you feel better, he's dead now. David ripped out his throat."

That was supposed to make her feel better? Case sure wasn't high on social skills.

"He's dead, I'm bitten, and David Vincent is free."

"Damn straight he's free," Shane fired. "You're the one who has been hanging around with the guy. Or do you think I didn't recognize you when you attacked us at the cabin? Your scent was the same, whether you're wearing the body of a gray wolf...or pretending to be human."

"I was undercover," Case gritted out. "I convinced David that I'd been working with Evan all along, that he could trust me and take me into his pack."

Olivia didn't know if she believed him. She wasn't about to put her trust in that man.

Olivia closed the distance between her and Chloe. "Are you in that pack?" Had she been so wrong about Chloe all this time?

"No!" Chloe grabbed her hands. "I-I can't even shift all of the way! I get stuck. I can't control the shifts and it's just...it's hell." A tear leaked down her cheek. "My dad tried to fix me, but he did something that made it all worse. I'd rather be a full werewolf than what I am now. Then at least I wouldn't live in fear *every second* that I'd lose my control and hurt someone."

Olivia wanted to believe her.

"David's pack is working for the senator."

Olivia glanced over at Case.

"I got in deep enough to learn that. The senator researched everything he could about your kind, Olivia, and he made sure you were pushed to your limits—so that the only way for you to survive was to bring out your djinn side."

Fire and blood.

Case hesitated, then said, "I think he killed your mother."

Shock rocked through Olivia. "Why would you say that? My mother died in a car accident when I was eighteen!"

"He tried to make her talk about you...about your father. He *made* her talk," Case corrected. "And the car accident was just the way to cover up her death."

Bile rose in Olivia's throat. She'd always thought that Donald was looking out for her.

"I've been working to bring that bastard down for a long time," Case continued. "Hell, you and I—we even crossed paths before when I was tailing him. I just got lucky because you didn't remember me when we met again at Purgatory."

No, no, she didn't remember him...

My mother? The senator killed my mother?

"I'm so sorry," Chloe whispered. "I didn't know...not until Case came to me and told me. *I didn't know, I swear!*"

She was going to be sick. Rage and pain and horror were swirling within Olivia.

She stumbled back, but Case caught her shoulders and stopped her retreat. "David got access to the senator's research. The senator trusts that wolf too damn much." He huffed out a breath. "You have to watch your emotions—they're the trigger for your power. When you lose control, that's when your magic is at its strongest. *That's what the senator wants.*"

For her to break? She tried to steady her racing heartbeat. "Where is the senator?"

Case glanced over at Chloe.

"Where is he?" Olivia demanded again.

"We don't know," Case confessed. "That's why we're here. We thought...we thought he'd be coming after you."

She pulled away from him and forced herself to look at Shane. "I guess there's a lot of that going around." Her chin lifted. "Shane, when you first sensed werewolves in the building, did you think it was David and his pack—coming for me? Coming to get the bait in your trap?"

His gaze held hers. "I knew it was Case."

"But you'd hoped it was the others?" She rushed back to the window. Stared down at the city below. "That's the whole point, right? Everyone is using me, manipulating me, and I'm so blind that I didn't realize it." Her laughter came then, and it was bitter. "I was supposed to be so good at reading people. I mean, I do it for a living! And the ones closest to me…" She looked at Chloe. At Shane. Pain tightened within her. "The ones closest to me deceived me the best."

Shane hurried toward her. "I didn't deceive you. I got you out of the Para Unit. You wanted to be free, and I made that happen."

She wasn't free. "Sometimes, you don't see the cage."

"The senator has to be stopped! David has to be caught or killed. It's not safe for the humans if they're still out there, plotting. It's not safe for you." He leaned in toward her, and she could see the fury swirling in his eyes. "I will do anything and everything to make your world safe, don't you see that? I would do—" He broke off and his gaze jerked toward the window. "No!" Shane yelled.

"What—"

Bullets blasted through the window, shattering the glass. Fast. One after the other. Shane grabbed her, pushed Olivia behind his body even as he faced the window, and she heard the terrible thudding impact as the bullets sank into him.

Chloe cried out as she was hit. Olivia's gaze flew to her, and she saw her friend jerking like a marionette on a string.

Case went down, crashing into the coffee table even as blood soaked his shirt.

The bullets kept firing. Shane was on his feet, still protecting Olivia even as his body shuddered. Then—

Silence.

The gunfire had stopped.

She wasn't hit. Shane…

He fell. His body slammed onto the floor, and he took her down with him. Olivia struggled with him and managed to roll him to the side. "Shane!"

There was blood everywhere, bullet wounds all over him. Her hand pressed to his chest.

That was when she realized there was a bullet in his heart.

"R-run…"

Olivia's head turned at that faint whisper. Chloe had tried to heave herself up a few precious inches. Blood soaked her shirt. "G-go…"

She was supposed to just leave them? Hell, *no*.

"S-silver in m-me…" Chloe shuddered. "Bet…w-wood…in v-vamp…"

A wooden bullet to the heart would put a vampire down. Freeze him, as if he were dead. She had to get the bullet out of Shane.

"C-coming…h-hear them…" Chloe fell back. "*Run…*"

She couldn't leave them!

She wouldn't leave Shane. Her fingers pushed into his wound, the wound right over his heart. She gasped as she did it, terrified, but Shane didn't move at all. Her fingers slipped, fumbled, and she tried to find that bullet. If she could get it out, then he'd wake up. He'd heal. Then they could grab the others and all get out of there.

If she could get the bullet… "Come on, come on…"

She heard the thunder of footsteps. So close. Right outside of the apartment?

Sucking in a deep breath, Olivia pushed her fingers even deeper into Shane's chest. She wouldn't think about touching his heart. She'd only think about saving him. Saving them all. She had to get the bullet out.

The door crashed in. She looked up as men in black rushed into the room. All of the men wore ski masks. She didn't know if they were humans or werewolves—they were in human form, though, and all armed with guns.

"Get away from him!"

That voice…she knew that voice. It was Donald Quick's voice.

He rushed right past his daughter's fallen form and put a gun to Olivia's head. "Get away from the vamp. Leave him or you die now!"

He had his gun aimed right between her eyes. "L-liar," Olivia said. "You want me alive." She almost had the bullet. Almost. "That's the whole point of all this, right, Senator Quick?"

He stiffened. What, had the guy thought she wouldn't recognize him? Or that she wouldn't call his bluff?

"You're right," he said softly. "I won't kill you." Then he backed away from her. Grabbed his daughter and jerked her upright. He put his gun to Chloe's head. "But what do you think will happen if I fire a silver bullet into her at point-blank range?"

Chloe's eyes were closed. She sagged in his hold.

"She's your daughter!" Olivia shouted.

"She turned on me. Who the hell do you think has been tipping off the FBI bastards? She turned on me...when all I wanted to do was help her." Rage blasted through his words. "Now get away from that vamp, or she dies!"

Olivia's fingers slowly slipped out of the wound. She put her hands behind her back as she rose.

"Good. Damn good." He dropped Chloe, as if she didn't matter at all. "Now, come on because we're leaving." He motioned with the gun. A "come here" gesture.

She didn't go anywhere. "Did you kill my mother?"

He tensed.

"You did." He'd been at her mother's funeral. Hugging Olivia. Comforting her. Rage pulsed through her. "You sonofabitch!" She lunged for him. "I wish—"

He shot her.

Olivia's words ended in a strangled gasp as she looked down at her body.

"Can't have you making any wishes, not just yet."

She saw the blood blooming near her stomach.

"Not fatal, not yet."

Her breath choked out as she staggered toward him. But one of his men rushed forward and shoved a needle into Olivia's neck.

"Got you," the man whispered. Her head turned as the world started to get foggy and dark, and she found herself staring into David's eerie silver eyes.

"I wish…" Olivia whispered, trying to force her words out. "I wish…"

She slumped to the floor.

And the bullet she'd hidden slipped from her fingers.

***

"Olivia!" Shane roared her name even as he sucked in a deep gulp of air. He lurched to his feet and slipped in blood. His blood.

Damn the bastards.

His gaze flew around the room. Case was on the floor, not moving at all. There was no sign of Olivia or Chloe. He inhaled, trying to pull in their scents and — *got you.*

He whirled back toward the window. The glass was broken, courtesy of the bullets and the sniper assholes who'd fired them. He looked below. Sure enough, there were black SUVs out there on the street. Olivia was being loaded into one.

I promised to protect her.

He jumped right through the glass. He plummeted down, down, and when he slammed into the ground, his knees dented the concrete.

"Kill him!" He heard the shouted order as he pushed to his feet. Men started firing at him again but, this time, they missed his heart.

He grabbed one of the fools. Yanked the guy in front of his body, used him as cover — and Shane sank his fangs into the man's throat.

He needed blood. He'd take everything from the bastards who'd tried to take Olivia.

When more bullets flew through the air, he dropped his prey. Shane went after the others. He'd take them all out. One by one.

A black SUV slammed into him. Shane hurtled through the air and hit the side of the building.

The SUV backed up.

Shane tried to shove to his feet. His legs were broken.

The SUV raced away.

And the men with guns closed in.

"I guess you're about to lose your head, vampire," one of the men yelled. "When we shoot you in your heart and you freeze up, do you think you'll still feel it when we saw off your head?"

Shane's hands flattened on the concrete. "Will you…feel it…when my friend…shoves his claws…into you?"

"What—?"

Connor attacked. Shane had smelled him, had known that back-up had come to help him. Connor ran up behind the men and sliced with his claws. One down. Two.

Then Duncan hurtled from the shadows. He took out two more men.

Pate rushed to Shane's side. "Damn, man, you look like hell." Pate put his wrist to Shane's mouth. "Haven't we done this shit before?"

Shane sank his teeth into Pate's wrist. The blood hit him, a punch of power, but it was nothing like the power boost he got from Olivia.

Olivia.

Shane shoved Pate's wrist away. He pushed his bones back into place and ignored the agony that pierced him.

He forced himself to rise. Shane took a step and managed to stay upright. Mostly. "They…took her."

"And we'll get her back," Pate promised. "She was bleeding so—"

"I've got her scent," Connor said at once as he dropped the guard he'd just clawed.

Shane staggered past them.

"You don't need her scent to track her," Pate said, coming up behind him. "Shane took her blood. There's nowhere she can go that he can't ever follow."

Nowhere. *I'd follow them to hell in order to get her back.* "Case...is upstairs." He hardly recognized his own growling voice. "Help him." Then he looked back at Pate. "And try to...keep up, with me."

You'll die for this, Senator Quick.

And Shane would make sure that it wouldn't be an easy death.

Olivia was his. Body, soul, heart. No one hurt her and lived.

The darkness that he kept chained so tightly took over and Shane started his hunt.

***

They'd gagged her. Tied up her hands. Bound her feet. And the senator kept a gun at her head as the SUV hurtled down the street.

"Are you angry, Olivia?" Donald asked as he leaned in close to her. "Are you afraid?"

She was *pissed,* and he should be the one who was afraid.

"I know all of your secrets. I know more than you can imagine."

She hated him. This, *this* was the man who'd attended all of her graduation ceremonies? Who'd been such a solid supporter in her life over the years?

He was using me, all along.

"Your father was a full-blood djinn. Your mother didn't realize that, though, not until it was too late. I actually think that part of her was always afraid of you. Afraid of what you might be."

No, no, her mother had *loved* her.

"She saw your father die. Vampires came after him...they like the taste of djinn blood, you see. The blood of a paranormal always gives them more power, but a djinn's blood — that's something quite special to them."

My vampire will come after me.

"The vampires came in full force and attacked your father. But he fought them. Took out most of those fanged bastards, slaughtered them, right in front of your mother. You were there, too, screaming." His lips twisted in a stark smile that was revealed by the faint light in the SUV. "At least, that's what she told me."

The SUV hit a pothole and the whole vehicle lurched.

She squeezed her eyes shut because she thought he might shoot her then. How easy would it be for that gun to discharge if the SUV hit another pothole that hard?

"Better move this," Donald murmured. "Don't want to accidently destroy all that magic."

That was all she was to him. Magic. Power.

But her eyes opened and she saw that he'd lowered the gun.

"Do you remember how he died?" Now he sounded curious.

Olivia shook her head.

"It was her," Donald whispered. "He'd fought the vamps. He was weak, and she killed him. Your mother thought he was evil. She'd seen what his wishes could do...watched as he twisted desires and played with the lives of humans. Your father — all djinn enjoy torment. Your mother knew he'd make you just like him, so she had to act."

Tears slipped down her cheeks. She wanted his words to be nothing more than lies but...

I don't think they are.

"Your powers were dormant. I knew I had to wake them, I just didn't know *how*." Now frustration thickened his words. "I sent you to killers. I put you face to face with evil, hoping it would trigger your own darkness."

He'd gotten her access to all of those serial killers in prison. She'd thought he wanted to help people, to *stop* death. But he'd just wanted to use her.

"But the humans weren't enough. They couldn't break through your wall. I'd met a shaman who told me that fear would be the key for breaking you."

So he'd sent her to Purgatory. *Opportunity of a lifetime, my ass.*

"Everyone fears the monsters there."

Olivia swallowed.

"But it still wasn't enough. So I had to try once more...all in," he murmured. "I thought...maybe what kills a djinn can make a djinn."

She glared at him.

"Blood and fire," he said.

The cabin. The werewolves.

"That woke you up, didn't it?" he whispered. "That woke up the beast that was sleeping in you. And now, that beast is *mine.*"

He thought he was going to control her?

He needed to think the hell again.

"You know the secret to controlling a djinn?" He put his hand on her chest. Right over her heart. "It's here."

The SUV stopped. Behind them, more headlights flashed. Another vehicle had pulled up behind them.

"You're going to grant my wishes, Olivia. You're going to give me everything that I want."

The SUV's door was opened. Donald shoved Olivia out. She hit the ground. The damn gag was still in place.

"Your power only works when you speak. So you're helpless now."

She heard a whimper. Olivia glanced over and saw Chloe being dragged out of the second SUV. Behind her gag, she shouted her friend's name.

A knife pressed to Olivia's chest. Right in the same spot that Donald had touched moments before. "I'm going to cut out your heart."

He was *insane!*

"Don't worry. You'll stay alive. The djinn do." He leaned toward her. Dropped his voice to a low murmur as he told her, "The hearts were kept in the bottles so long ago. That's where the real power was. Control a djinn's heart, control a djinn's power. I *will* control you." He smiled at her, the smile glinted in the darkness, and she realized that his teeth were too sharp. And his eyes were almost glowing.

The senator was a werewolf. Had he been born that way? And passed the DNA of a paranormal on down to his daughter? That would explain how Chloe had survived her attack as a teen. Or maybe...had the senator been bitten at some point, too?

"You're going to give me more power than anyone else has ever possessed. The world will be *mine.*"

Olivia realized that how the guy had become a werewolf didn't matter—not then. All that mattered was that he was the enemy, and she couldn't let him win. The blade of the knife cut into her. Olivia twisted, shoving out with her feet, and she hit the senator in the stomach. He grunted and staggered back. She took that opportunity and rolled, as fast and hard as she could. She would get away. Somehow. That bastard wasn't cutting out her heart!

The blade sliced over her arm. He grabbed her legs. "Soon, you'll never fight me again."

She'd fight him until she died.

"*Get your fucking hands off her!*"

Shane's voice. Shane's wonderful roar of rage.

Then he was there, yanking the senator back, tossing him away from her. Shane reached for her legs. Ripped the rope away. He caught her hands and jerked—

A white werewolf—fully shifted—tackled him. Shane tumbled to the ground, rolling with that beast. The wolf sank his teeth into Shane's neck.

She twisted and yanked her hands as she struggled to get out of the rope. The rope wasn't giving, so—*screw it*. Olivia contorted her body as best she could. Her shoulder popped, and she knew she'd dislocated it, but she managed to get her hands around her bunched up legs so that her bound hands weren't behind her anymore. They were in front of her, and she could reach her gag.

She grabbed for the gag just as Shane locked his fingers around the werewolf's jaws.

Shane pried the jaws off him.

Olivia yanked out her gag.

"I wish the beast would be a man!"

The werewolf shifted before her, changing instantly. The white fur melted. His bones snapped and popped. Shane lost his grip on the werewolf—*a man now*—and David curled into a ball on the ground.

David was completely naked and—*sobbing?*

"You fucking killed him!" David yelled as he tipped back his head and glared at her. "I felt it—*you killed my beast!*"

The senator had gotten back to his feet. He also had his knife—now pressed over his daughter's heart.

"Lost it," David muttered as he rocked back and forth. "Lost my beast, *lost my beast!*"

Shane, bleeding but still standing, crossed to Olivia's side. He tore the ropes away from her raw wrists even as he kept his glare on David. "Guess that means you aren't an alpha any longer."

Shane was looking at the wrong threat. "I wish you'd let her go," Olivia said to Donald.

He nodded. "Right…" His voice was soft. "I will…*let her go…*"

And he shoved the knife into his daughter's chest.

Olivia screamed as Chloe fell to the ground.

"I let her go," Donald whispered.

Horror froze Olivia. Too late, she remembered that a djinn's wishes were twisted. What had she been told? That they could turn dreams into nightmares?

She'd just killed Chloe! "I wish she was alive!" The words tumbled from her in a frantic shout. "I wish—"

"Olivia, *no!*" Shane grabbed her and held tight. "Stop it! He's pushing you! Manipulating you!"

But Chloe was moving now. Gasping. Shuddering. *Alive.*

"You are as strong as they say," Donald murmured, with a flash of his fangs. "How fucking wonderful."

Another vehicle raced to the scene. A big, black van. The driver's side opened and Pate leapt out. Connor and Duncan jumped out, too, and they rushed toward the senator.

David kept whimpering on the ground. *"Lost my beast, lost…"*

"It's over, senator." Pate's voice rang out, strong and clear. "You're done."

"Oh? And here I thought I was just getting started…"

Olivia had clamped her lips together. She wanted to make another wish. Wanted it so badly.

But it was a dark wish. Evil.

I shouldn't wish for a man's death.

"They've been using you, Olivia," Donald called out as Pate and Connor closed in on him. Duncan stalked toward David. "I told you…the way to control a djinn is through the heart. I would've kept your heart safe, but what do you think the vampire will do to it?"

Shane's arms tightened around her.

"His family is corrupt. They've bathed in blood for centuries. Do you know how many innocents your lover slaughtered? He and his family—they're the reason vampires exist today. The reason so many humans hunt and kill."

Pate yanked the bloody knife from Donald's hand. "Guess where you're going, senator? I'm glad you liked Purgatory so much because it's going to be your new home."

Donald didn't look at him. His eyes were on Olivia. "He didn't even have to cut out your heart in order to control you. All the vampire had to do was make you love him. You *gave* him your heart, and he'll use it. He'll use your power. You'll do anything, everything, he wants now, and you'll be helpless."

Pate locked his hands around the senator's shoulder, but Donald jerked away from him.

"They've all been using you!" He screamed at Olivia.

She kept her mouth closed. *Don't wish his death...don't!*

"The vampire marked you because he wanted that power for himself! He doesn't love you, he's just screwing you for —"

Shane rushed at the senator. He grabbed the man's shirt. Lifted him high into the air. "You were going to cut out her heart!"

The senator smiled. "One day, I will," he promised. "I'll come back. I won't stop, I'll have everything —"

"You'll have nothing." Then Shane sank his teeth into the senator's throat. Donald howled and slashed out at Shane with his claws. He punched and twisted, but Shane didn't let him go.

He kept drinking. Kept taking.

Kept...killing?

"Stop," Olivia whispered.

Shane instantly stilled.

"Send him to Purgatory," she said, her voice weak, but determined. Because death would be too easy for that bastard. "Let the prisoners there torture him." *You can see what it's like to be locked up with them.*

Shane dropped the senator to the ground. Donald didn't move as the blood gushed from his throat. He didn't move...at first.

Then he started to laugh. The laugh was rough and broken, and evil. "I...made Purgatory. My monsters...planning to attack. They won't hurt me." He pushed to his feet. "We'll be stronger. We'll never stop! No one will ever stop *me* – "

"I will," Chloe said. She was on her feet, too, swaying. She lifted her hands and Olivia saw that her friend had grabbed a gun. A gun that she must have taken from one of the downed guards. "Goodbye, daddy." She fired the weapon.

The bullet slammed into the senator.

"Silver," Shane muttered. "Straight to the heart."

The senator fell then, his face slack with surprise.

Chloe dropped the gun. "He was a monster," she said, pain heavy in her voice, "long before he became a werewolf."

CHAPTER TWELVE

"She can't just run loose out in the world, Shane." Pate was seated behind his desk, and currently sweating one hell of a lot. "She's too dangerous."

Shane leaned forward. He was done with the Para Unit...for now. He had other plans. Other priorities. Priority one was Olivia. But Pate had taken her back into custody, and that shit just wasn't flying for Shane. "You found the senator's Intel on her."

Pate nodded. "Her wishes...she can wreck the world. There is no limit to her power. If she speaks it, it happens. Only her wishes twist up and can *hurt* thousands. With a djinn, no wish is a simple matter—they are *all* dark."

Shane's eyes narrowed. "Olivia isn't evil."

"No, dammit, I know she's not." Pate yanked a hand through his hair. "It's all about her and her emotions. Don't you see that? If she's happy, then freaking fantastic—her wishes will come out good and smooth and millions won't die." His chair squeaked as he leaned forward. "But if she's scared...if she's angry...if someone pisses her off, then her wishes are designed to wreck and punish. It's the way of the djinn—"

"That's not Olivia. She's not evil," he said again. Olivia was the best thing that had ever happened to him.

"She's not," Pate agreed once more, but he paused. Pate swallowed as his eyelids flickered. Then he slowly asked, "But are you?"

Really, the SOB had just gone there?

"Because the senator was right," Pate said. "*You* don't have to cut out her heart to control that woman. I saw the way she looks at you. She's half in love with you already. And according to the senator's research, a djinn *has* to grant the wishes of the person he or she loves. Hell, that's why Olivia's father didn't kill her when she was a kid and he went on that rampage. Her mother wished for Olivia's safety, for her protection."

Shane didn't like where this was going.

"I know what you've done," Pate spoke quietly, the words low and intense. "And I know what you *could* do. Are you seriously telling me that you trust yourself with her? Can you promise me that you'd never use her?"

His back teeth ground together. "I only want her safe. Happy."

Pate shoved to his feet. "Right. That's the damn problem. You want her happy so you wish there would never be a threat to her." Pate snapped his fingers together. "Boom…your girl just took out all the werewolves in existence."

Shane rose, slowly.

"Some bitch in a store says something catty to Olivia one day, and you wish the chick would shut her mouth…" Pate snapped his fingers again. "Boom…that woman doesn't have a mouth. She can never talk."

"I wouldn't wish—"

"Donald found some damn shaman who told him that when a djinn mates—truly mates—she doesn't even have to hear her lover's wishes. She can feel his emotions. She grants all that he desires." Pate lifted his hand, his fingers poised to snap once more. "So if—"

Shane grabbed his hand. "Don't."

A muscle jerked in Pate's jaw. "It's not even her voice that gives power to the wish. She just has to *think* it." He stared into Shane's eyes. "Go ask her if she wished for Donald's death, because I think she did. Chloe can't even remember attacking her father. She doesn't remember anything that happened to her after Donald shoved that silver knife in her chest."

Shane glanced away from him. "So what the hell are you suggesting we do with Olivia? Keep her locked up? Forever?"

"That's an option."

Shane grabbed his friend and pinned him to the wall. "The hell it is. No one cages her."

Pate swallowed.

"What's the second option?"

Pate didn't speak.

Shane leaned in close. "You better not be fucking thinking death."

"I-I didn't realize how powerful she'd be — we have to stop the djinn inside of her..." Pate shook his head. "There's a reason the djinn were killed off. Because if they're not taken out, they'll destroy the rest of us!"

He nearly destroyed Pate in that moment. "No one will hurt her. I won't let that happen."

Pate's laugh was strangled. "She...doesn't need you for protection. She's got all her powers now. The woman could kill us all right at this moment, and we'd never have the chance to fight."

"Not now," Shane snarled. "Because you have her in a cell, caged with your damn blood marks!"

"It's the only thing keeping her in check!"

Shane bared his fangs.

"Man..." Now fear entered Pate's voice. "It's me. *Me.* I'm your friend."

"And she's everything. *Everything* to me." He was far too close to attacking Pate. Shane forced himself to step back. To *think*.

There had to be a way out of this mess. A way that didn't involve losing Olivia. A way that would let them stay together, forever.

Forever...

He smiled.

"You're going to kill me," Pate said, sounding utterly certain.

"Not yet," Shane told him. "But you'd better stop tempting me." He whirled away. Headed for the door.

"Where are you going?" Pate yelled.

"To offer Olivia forever, if she'll have me."

"*What?*"

Shane slammed the door shut behind him.

***

Her cell door flew open. Olivia jumped to her feet, and when she saw Shane rushing toward her, happiness seemed to explode within her. She grabbed him, wrapped her arms around him, and held tight.

She wouldn't have long with him. She knew that. Olivia had figured out the fate that waited for her already. So she'd hold him and enjoy him while she could.

He kissed her. His mouth was desperate and hungry on hers. She couldn't get close enough to him. His taste, his touch. She needed him so much.

"It's all right," Shane whispered against her mouth. "Everything is going to be all right."

Her vampire was such a liar. There was no way things could be all right.

Olivia knew exactly what she'd done.

She'd raised the dead.

She'd forced a daughter to kill her own father. Just with a thought.

I just wished he'd die. That he'd feel the same betrayal I felt.

And then Chloe had acted.

I'm sorry, Chloe.

Shane pulled back a bit. Stared into her eyes. "You are the most beautiful thing I've ever seen."

"And the most dangerous?" Olivia asked, voice breaking a bit. It was almost funny. She'd once interviewed monsters, never realizing that she was the biggest threat out there.

Shane caught her hands in his. Stared down at her. Emotions swirled in his gaze.

She dared to ask, "Pate plans to keep me locked up, doesn't he?"

Shane didn't answer.

"It...it's probably the safest idea. Until I can learn to control myself." *If* she could. Olivia wasn't sure it was possible. No...no, *be honest.* "I won't ever control myself. I can feel it...the power inside. Like a black hole that's stretching and trying to take me over."

Shane shouldn't be there with her. She wanted him close because—he'd gotten to her. Broken through her armor and reached the woman inside. Love shouldn't happen so quickly.

But then, wishes shouldn't go dark, either.

Life wasn't fair. It was twisted—as twisted as her wishes—hard and cold. And beautiful. Sometimes, so beautiful and good.

She wanted to remember the good times. When she spent years caged up, the good memories would be all that she had.

"It won't take you over." He sounded so confident.

He didn't understand that it already had. She'd killed, with just a thought.

But then Shane lowered before her, bowing down on his knees.

Olivia shook her head and blinked in confusion. "What are you doing?"

"I know you don't believe in mates, but do you think you could believe in me? In us?" His hands held hers. "Because I do. And I pledge myself to you. Right here. Right now. I pledge that I will always be by your side. I will stay with you through any danger that comes. I will celebrate with you, and I will mourn with you."

His words seemed to wrap around her.

"I will tie my life with yours."

Those words…it almost seemed like some kind of ceremony that he was performing. "What are you doing?"

"Being with you, if you'll have me."

She wanted no one else.

He stared up at her. "I love you."

Olivia shook her head.

"I wasn't manipulating you. Wasn't trying to seduce you into giving me your delectable body and, apparently, your all-powerful heart. I just wanted you. I needed you. And I would have done anything to have you."

She would have done anything to have him. But it wasn't just about what she wanted. It wasn't safe for him to be with her. It wasn't safe for anyone to be with her. "You should go." She had to blink away tears. *I have to keep him safe. He's only safe when he's away from me. Everyone is safe…away from me.*

He stayed on his knees, and he shook his head.

"Pate won't let me out." He had to see that.

His lips thinned, and then Shane said, "We have two options."

Her heart slammed into her chest.

"If you stay locked up, then I stay with you."

No, that *couldn't* happen.

"It won't be Purgatory. It will be paradise, because I'll be with you."

"Bullshit," Olivia instantly called.

His lips twitched.

"It will be prison," Olivia said, "and I won't have that for you."

His hold tightened on her hands. "Then that gives us option two."

She wasn't so sure she wanted to hear this one.

"The djinn dies."

Olivia tried to pull away, but he wouldn't let her go. "You're...going to kill me?"

"I want you alive forever, Olivia. I don't want to think of any world without you in it." His gaze fell to her neck. "I can make you something other than djinn."

And she understood. "Vampire."

He nodded. "I've taken your blood. You know the pleasure to be found there."

It was rather hard to forget that particular pleasure.

"If you drink from me, I can change you. Your human side will die, and your djinn side...it will either die, too, and you'll become a full vampire..."

He trailed off. She waited. And waited a bit more. "Shane?"

"Or something else could happen." His words were gruff. "When Holly gave her blood to Duncan, he became a blend of vampire and werewolf. You could change like that, too. Then you would —"

"I'd have the immortality of a vampire and the power of a djinn! Isn't that rather like unleashing hell on earth?"

He surged to his feet. "Maybe you will be both, but maybe you'll have control then! Maybe your djinn powers will be muted and the wishes won't twist!"

"Or maybe they'll be even darker." Vamps weren't exactly known for being all sweetness and light. More like known for being bloodthirsty and brutal.

"If that happens, then we keep you locked up." His voice was soft. "And I stay with you."

"Both of these options suck!" She glanced toward the video camera that had been mounted on the right wall. "Are these Pate's options?" They sure sounded like him.

"He wants to keep you caged. Or he just wants to kill you. No transformation. Just death."

Her heart stuttered in her chest. "Blood and fire."

"That's *not* happening." He grabbed her. Pulled Olivia against him and kissed her. Deep and hard and long. "We are going to have forever. Say yes, Olivia, just say yes to my bite, to the exchange, and give us a chance."

She wanted to, but Olivia was terrified.

"If something goes wrong," he rasped, "you're still here, locked up. You won't hurt anyone."

Unless her power strengthened too much for the markings on the floor to hold her in check. *Don't call them markings anymore. You know it's a spell. Some magic that Pate is working.*

Which meant Pate was way past human.

So am I.

"Unless you don't...want to be with me." He cleared his throat. "I can still change you, then you can walk away from me. You don't have to —"

"I'd like to spend all of my days and nights with you." The truth. Her deepest wi —

She cut that thought off.

"Then you want my bite? My blood?"

Olivia took a deep breath. There was no going back to a normal life. And there might be no going to a *vampire* life either. But she wanted to try because she wanted Shane. "I want you," she said simply.

Then she tilted her head to the side and offered him her neck. His head bent. His breath brushed over her skin. Olivia closed her eyes. When his teeth pierced her, the pleasure rose within her, hot and strong. So overwhelming. Pushing the fear back. Pushing the memory of death from her mind.

He lifted her into his arms. Carried her toward the wall, the one just beneath that video camera. *Pate won't see us here.*

Her body shuddered against his. His mouth...his tongue...

His teeth left her. "I have to take a lot more blood this time." His words vibrated against her. "Just trust me, love. I'll keep you safe."

She did trust him. With every bit of her soul.

His teeth pierced her again and he drank. Pleasure came, rising and quaking through her body. Pleasure that came again and again, climaxes that left her shaken because one just tumbled into another.

The pleasure was so good that soon all she could do was sag in his hold. Her hands slid to her sides, not touching him any longer. She was weak with pleasure...*weak.*

Then his head lifted and he stared down at her once more. He had her pinned to the wall, and she felt his arousal shoving against her. As she stared into his eyes, Olivia saw so many emotions.

Desire. Fear. Need.

But most of all, love.

Staring at her, he lifted his wrist toward his mouth. The dragon tattoo circled that wrist. *If hell breaks loose, look for a dragon.* Pate's words whispered through her mind.

He used his teeth to rake over the flesh. Then he offered the drops of blood to her.

"Take all that I am," he told her.

He put his wrist to her mouth. His blood flowed onto her tongue. Powerful. Rich. So strong.

And the weakness that she'd felt vanished. Lust pumped through her, a dark and wild desire that seemed to claw through her body. Her hands locked on his shoulders. Her nails dug into his skin as she fought to get ever closer to him and she kept drinking from his wrist. She—

"*What the hell are you doing?*" Pate yelled. He was in the doorway, glaring at them. "You can't change her! She'll be unstoppable then!"

Shane snarled and turned away from her, putting his body in front of Olivia's. Without his blood, without his touch, she felt bereft.

"Stay back," Shane ordered Pate. "Or I'll put you into the ground...and you won't rise this time."

This time?

Her stomach knotted. A convulsive shudder shook her. Olivia looked down and saw that her fingers were trembling. "Sh-Shane...?" She swayed, slipping to the side.

Connor pushed his way into the room, knocking Pate out of his way. His fierce glance took in the scene, including Shane's bleeding wrist. He gave a low whistle. "Trying to turn her? Good plan, man—"

"It's not a good plan!" Pate shouted. "She's not you! She's not Duncan! *She's not a werewolf!* Look at the power boost you two got. What the hell do you think will happen to her?"

She couldn't feel her legs. "Shane..."

His head snapped toward her.

"Am I s-supposed to be so cold?"

He scooped her into his arms. "Love?"

Pain racketed her. The pleasure was gone. Something was *wrong*. But Olivia found that she could somehow smile. For him. "I do...love you..."

Another shudder rocked her. *No, I'm not shuddering – I'm seizing.*

Her heart didn't seem to beat. Her blood...everything within her felt so *still*.

Olivia realized she wasn't breathing any longer. She wasn't blinking. She could hear. She could see. But she was frozen.

Dead?

"*Olivia!*" Shane put his wrist to her mouth. "You just need more blood. That's all. You'll be fine."

She didn't taste his blood. She didn't taste anything. And even though her eyes were open, it was becoming harder to see.

When you die...what's the last sense that you lose? That stupid fucking question ran through her mind.

Hearing.

Because she could hear everything happening around her, but she couldn't speak. Couldn't see. Couldn't feel. She was wishing then, wishing desperately that she could live. If she had any magic left, any power, she just wanted to live.

To be with Shane. To see what their future could be like. He'd made her happy. Made her feel safe. For such a precious time, he'd even made her hope.

But...

She couldn't hear him any longer.

She couldn't see anything. Couldn't feel anything. Couldn't hear anything.

I love you, Shane.

***

"We need Holly in here, *now!*" Pate bellowed. Then he locked his hands around Shane and tried to pull him away from Olivia.

That shit wasn't happening. Shane shoved him back. "Olivia, love, please, open your eyes!" This wasn't supposed to happen. He'd transformed others over the centuries. This had never happened.

Her convulsions had stopped. Her eyes were closed. Her chest still. She wasn't breathing. Wasn't moving at all.

He kept trying to give her more of his blood. If she just took more, she'd be all right. She had to be all right.

Connor grabbed him. So did Duncan. He fought them, twisting and punching with all his might. No one could take him from Olivia!

"Holly may be able to help her!" Pate shouted. "Dammit, man, we are your friends, stop. *Stop!*"

And he realized that he was strangling Duncan.

Shane heaved out a breath. One. Two. His fingers loosened on Duncan as Holly rushed to Olivia's side.

Holly felt for Olivia's pulse. "What happened to her?"

"I was…" His voice was hollow. Broken. "I was going to change her."

"Take him out of here," Pate ordered Connor and Duncan. "Get him out, *now!* Take him to the yard."

Shane shook his head. He lunged toward Olivia.

But Pate was in his path.

"I can't find a pulse," Holly said, voice sharp.

No, *no*.

Pate put his hands on Shane's chest. "Holly needs room to work. Go to the yard. Wait for us."

"I can save her!" He had to save her.

Sympathy flashed on Pate's face. "No, Shane, you can't. If you could, then she'd be breathing right now."

Olivia couldn't be dead. She couldn't. And he wasn't leaving her. His control broke as he roared for her. He leapt forward, determined to touch her. To get to her.

But the others swarmed in on him. Pate. Connor. Duncan. They dragged him out of there, even as he fought. Holly was bent over Olivia, but Olivia still hadn't moved.

"I wish you'd stay with me!" Shane shouted out, desperate. "I wish you'd never leave me!"

"Dammit, man, don't say shit like that!" Connor growled. "With the way those djinn wishes work, you'd wind up with a zombie bride."

His friends weren't letting him go. No matter how much he hurt them. "I just want her."

Then they were outside, in the area known as the "yard" at the facility. A high, chain-length fence surrounded them—that fence was laced with silver. The moon shone down on them, too bright.

He heaved the others off him. Turned to rush back inside.

"If she can be saved," Pate said softly, "Holly will save her. Holly's a doctor—give her a chance!"

Medicine wasn't enough.

"Give her a chance," Pate urged again.

Shane's hands were fisted at his sides. "What will I do if she dies?"

Pate didn't speak.

Is she already dead? Did I kill her? The one woman that I wanted the most?

He truly was a monster, and right then, he was in hell.

CHAPTER THIRTEEN

Olivia's eyes opened as she sucked in a deep gulp of air. She blinked and saw Holly only an inch away from her.

Holly's jaw dropped. "You're alive!"

Of course, she was alive.

Holly scrambled back. "You were stone cold dead!"

Right, well, didn't that happen when you became a vampire? Olivia wasn't quite clear on the whole transformation bit, but vamps had to be called the *un*dead for some reason.

"Where's Shane?" She pushed off the floor. She felt good. Better than good. Amazingly strong.

Amazingly hungry.

Holly inched back. "He's outside."

He'd left her? Not cool.

"Olivia...what are you?"

Olivia wasn't too sure on that score herself. "Let's find out." She headed toward the red markings on the floor. Bracing herself, she lifted her foot to walk over them. Maybe she'd slam into the invisible wall again or maybe —

She just walked right over the red lines. Olivia laughed. "It worked!"

"Did it?" Holly sounded unsure. Worried.

A big smile broke over Olivia's face. "The spell doesn't hold me in check anymore! I'm free!"

"Or just even stronger." Holly bit her lip. "You should...you should make a wish. See what happens."

Her heart stuttered. "What if it goes wrong?" Now she was the one who sounded unsure.

Holly swallowed. "Make a wish."

Something that isn't dangerous. Something that won't backfire on me. Or on anyone else. "I wish it would rain."

That was an easy enough wish, right?

Holly stared back at her. Then she looked up at the ceiling. Nothing.

Well, at least rain wasn't falling magically from the ceiling.

"Outside," Holly murmured. "We should check outside."

Olivia was already ahead of her. She sprang for the doorway, so eager to be out of her prison. She ran down the hallway and then realized she was following a particular scent. *His* scent. Rich and masculine and sexy.

And she could hear Shane. The faint rumble of his voice. Even though he was outside of the building, she could still *hear* him.

She had a vampire's senses.

Olivia threw open the exterior door. Stumbled into the area she'd heard the others call the "yard" before. The men whirled toward her.

She ignored Pate and Duncan and Connor. Even though they were all staring at her like she was some kind of freak.

"Zombie bride," she heard Connor mutter. "Please, don't be..."

"Shane," she whispered, and she smiled at him. "It's not raining."

In the next second, he had her in his arms. His mouth crashed down on hers and it was wonderful. Fantastic. Fabulous. His body was strong and hard against hers, and it wasn't raining.

Her wish hadn't come true.

Her tongue slid over his lips. Pushed into his mouth. Adrenaline and desire and euphoria were swirling within her.

So was something else...

Her mouth pulled from his. Olivia's teeth were burning. Stretching. Yes, she had a vampire's senses. She also had a vampire's hunger and that bloodlust was growing within her.

Shane stared down at her mouth. Then, slowly, his gaze lifted to her eyes. A wide smile split his face. "It worked!"

She wanted his blood.

She wanted him.

Forever.

"I don't think she's a djinn any longer," Holly said from behind them. "He changed her."

"No," Shane said as he kept staring into Olivia's eyes. "She changed me. She changed everything, for me."

In his hot stare, Olivia could see his desire and his love.

"I thought I'd lost you," he whispered.

For a minute there — or longer — Olivia had thought she was lost, too.

"Uh, yeah…a newly turned vamp will need to feed," Connor said. "We should um…give them some privacy."

Shane didn't look away from her. "Yes, you fucking should."

She heard the others retreat inside. The door shut — very loudly — behind them. Olivia ran her tongue over the edge of her new fangs. "I want to taste you."

"Love, I'm yours…"

She pushed him back, and he hit the tall, heavy fence. Olivia grabbed his shirt because now that they were alone, she couldn't hold back.

She'd always been told that physical lust and bloodlust mixed for vampires. It was sure mixing for her.

His shirt tore beneath her hands.

He laughed.

She *loved* his laugh. Olivia rose onto her tip-toes. She pressed a kiss to his throat. *So good.* She licked him. His pulse was racing, and it should be awkward, she should be hesitating — but her teeth sank into him so easily.

So simply. So perfectly.

His blood flowed onto her tongue. Rich, but strangely sweet. Like a fine chocolate. She *loved* chocolate.

He groaned, a ragged, desperate sound.

Olivia immediately jerked her mouth away. "Did I hurt you?"

His eyes opened.

No, that's not pain.

"Pleasure, love, only pleasure." And then he was the one to catch her in his arms. He pulled her close. Lifted her up.

Olivia wrapped her legs around him, and when his teeth sank into her throat—

It was just as it had been before. A powerful surge of pleasure rushed through her whole body. Incredible.

She pushed her sex against him. Their clothes were in the way. She wanted to be naked. She didn't care where they were. She had to be with him.

This time, her back hit the fence. He let her go just long enough to strip away her jeans and to yank open his pants. Then he lifted her up again. Her legs curled tightly around him.

"Hold on," he told her.

"Always," she promised.

His fingers twined in that fence, gripping tightly on either side of her head, then he surged into her. Filling her so deeply, so completely.

He thrust, driving into her once, twice, surging right over her clit—

She bit him.

They both came, erupting with a wild fury that didn't end. A fury that churned through Olivia, pulsating through every inch of her body. So powerful. So complete.

So perfect.

When it ended, finally, aftershocks still had her sex contracting around him. She licked his throat, trying to soothe the small wound that she'd left there.

She'd marked him.

Just as he'd marked her.

Shane's head lifted. He stared into her eyes. "I love you."

"I love you, too." After all, she wouldn't have sex up against a fence with just any guy. Only Shane. Forever...*Shane*.

"Always," he said as his lips brushed against hers.

It was a promise for them. Hope for the future.

"Always," Olivia whispered back.

And a light mist began to fall on them. Soft rain that drizzled down from the night sky.

She tensed in his arms.

He kissed her again. "It's okay. It's just a little rain."

Olivia shook her head. What if it wasn't just rain? What if it was more?

"It's just rain," he said again, his eyes dark and determined as he gazed at her. "It can't hurt us. Nothing can hurt us. Not anymore."

I wish the rain would stop. She had that thought, so clearly in her mind.

And the rain grew harder as it pelted down on them.

"I wish the rain would stop," Olivia shouted.

It didn't. It soaked them. Poured and lightning flashed.

She laughed then. Laughed and held tight to her vampire lover. The darkness inside of her didn't seem like a dangerous, crouching beast any longer. It seemed...natural. A part of her that could be controlled.

She tilted back her head and let the rain fall on her. The past washed away. All of the fear. All of the death. The rain washed it all away.

The future waited for her now.

Forever.

What more could a woman wish for?

EPILOGUE

The rain had stopped.

Eric stood at his window, staring out at the night.

Shane had taken Olivia away. He wasn't sure where they'd gone. When a vampire as powerful as Shane wanted to vanish, stopping him wasn't exactly an easy thing to do.

Especially if I wanted to keep him on my side.

If he'd battled Shane, tried to keep Olivia there longer for tests, hell, he might very well have lost his head.

That tended to happen to Shane's enemies.

"So...she's not a djinn any longer?" Connor asked carefully. "She's a vampire?"

"She's not a threat any longer." That was the only thing he was willing to say. "But others are." He turned toward the werewolf in front of him. "I need your help."

Connor shrugged. "Well, seeing as how you're the guy who keeps me from getting tossed *into* Purgatory, you know I'll do what you want." His jaw hardened. "I kind of fucking have to."

Because Connor wasn't a man with a clean past. He was trying to earn his redemption, the same way that Shane had.

"Case is going to be out of commission for a while." That was putting things mildly, but at least the guy would survive. Eric had plans for him, too. "You have to take his place."

Connor raised his brows. "Just where was his place?"

"I need you to guard Chloe Quick."

Surprise flashed across Connor's face. "The senator's daughter? But the senator is dead! He's no threat to her any longer."

"He's not. But others out there are."

Connor leaned toward him. "You need to find someone else for this mission."

"I need a *werewolf* for this one. Your kind isn't exactly running loose and wild at the FBI."

"I can't be her babysitter. I can't be—" He broke off, and when he spoke again, his words were stilted. Too controlled. "I don't think it's a good idea for me to be in close proximity with her."

Now that was interesting. "Why not?"

Connor looked away.

"You can keep your control on a mission, can't you, Connor?"

"Yes," he snapped.

"Because I need you," Eric continued. "I need a werewolf close to Chloe. The senator wasn't working alone. There was a whole damn pack who attacked us at the cabin. We need to destroy that pack, and find out just what end goal that group has."

Connor stood. "I don't do so well in a pack."

Right. The guy was more of a lone wolf, but he was also an alpha. If anyone could get the job done, it would be him. "Finish this mission, and the slate is wiped clean. As far as the government is concerned, all of the sins from your past will be wiped away."

Surprise flashed on Connor's face. "I'd be done? Clear with the FBI?"

"Provided," Eric added carefully, "that you manage to keep Chloe Quick alive for the course of this mission." He leaned forward. "She's important. An asset that we can't lose or compromise anymore. Do you understand?"

A slow nod was his answer. Then Connor said, "I understand. I can keep her alive, but you need to understand something, too."

Eric lifted a brow.

"I'll keep her alive, but as soon as this mission is over…" He flashed a smile, one that showed wickedly sharp teeth. "I'll have my freedom, and Uncle Sam can kiss my ass."

Eric offered his hand. "Deal."

Connor shook his hand and then left the room. When the door shut behind him, Eric sighed.

Sometimes, he really hated lying to his friends.

###

A NOTE FROM THE AUTHOR

Thank you so much for taking the time to read MARKED BY THE VAMPIRE. I hope that you enjoyed Shane and Olivia's story. If you haven't read the first book in the Purgatory series, THE WOLF WITHIN, that story is available now. And I am also working on the third book in the series, CHARMING THE BEAST (due out later in 2014).

If you'd like to stay updated on my releases and sales, please join my newsletter www.cynthiaeden.com/newsletter/. You can also check out my Facebook page www.facebook.com/cynthiaedenfanpage. I love to post giveaways over at Facebook!

Again, thank you for reading my story.

Best,

Cynthia Eden

www.cynthiaeden.com

COMING IN OCTOBER 2014…

CHARMING THE BEAST

(A Purgatory Novel) – Connor's Story

The big, bad beast is about to meet his match.

HER WORKS

Paraonormal romances by Cynthia Eden:

- BOUND BY BLOOD (Bound, Book 1)
- BOUND IN DARKNESS (Bound, Book 2)
- BOUND IN SIN (Bound, Book 3)
- BOUND BY THE NIGHT (Bound, Book 4)
- *FOREVER BOUND - An anthology containing: BOUND BY BLOOD, BOUND IN DARKNESS, BOUND IN SIN, AND BOUND BY THE NIGHT
- BOUND IN DEATH (Bound, Book 5)

- THE WOLF WITHIN (Purgatory, Book 1)
- MARKED BY THE VAMPIRE (Purgatory, Book 2)
- CHARMING THE BEAST (Purgatory, Book 3) - Available October 2014

Other paranormal romances by Cynthia Eden:

- A VAMPIRE'S CHRISTMAS CAROL
- BLEED FOR ME

- BURN FOR ME (Phoenix Fire, Book 1)
- ONCE BITTEN, TWICE BURNED (Phoenix Fire, Book 2)
- PLAYING WITH FIRE (Phoenix Fire, Book 3)

- ANGEL OF DARKNESS (Fallen, Book 1)
- ANGEL BETRAYED (Fallen, Book 2)
- ANGEL IN CHAINS (Fallen, Book 3)
- AVENGING ANGEL (Fallen, Book 4)

- IMMORTAL DANGER
- NEVER CRY WOLF
- A BIT OF BITE (Free Read!!)

- ETERNAL HUNTER (Night Watch, Book 1)
- I'LL BE SLAYING YOU (Night Watch, Book 2)
- ETERNAL FLAME (Night Watch, Book 3)

- HOTTER AFTER MIDNIGHT (Midnight, Book 1)
- MIDNIGHT SINS (Midnight, Book 2)
- MIDNIGHT'S MASTER (Midnight, Book 3)

- WHEN HE WAS BAD (anthology)
- EVERLASTING BAD BOYS (anthology)
- BELONG TO THE NIGHT (anthology)

List of Cynthia Eden's romantic suspense titles:

- MINE TO TAKE (Mine, Book 1)
- MINE TO KEEP (Mine, Book 2)
- MINE TO HOLD (Mine, Book 3)
- MINE TO CRAVE (Mine, Book 4)

- FIRST TASTE OF DARKNESS
- SINFUL SECRETS

- DIE FOR ME (For Me, Book 1)
- FEAR FOR ME (For Me, Book 2)
- SCREAM FOR ME (For Me, Book 3)

- DEADLY FEAR (Deadly, Book 1)
- DEADLY HEAT (Deadly, Book 2)
- DEADLY LIES (Deadly, Book 3)

- ALPHA ONE (Shadow Agents, Book 1)
- GUARDIAN RANGER (Shadow Agents, Book 2)
- SHARPSHOOTER (Shadow Agents, Book 3)
- GLITTER AND GUNFIRE (Shadow Agents, Book 4)
- UNDERCOVER CAPTOR (Shadow Agents, Book 5)
- THE GIRL NEXT DOOR (Shadow Agents, Book 6)
- EVIDENCE OF PASSION (Shadow Agents, Book 7)
- WAY OF THE SHADOWS (Shadow Agents, Book 8)

ABOUT THE AUTHOR

Award-winning author Cynthia Eden writes dark tales of paranormal romance and romantic suspense. She is a New York Times, USA Today, Digital Book World, and IndieReader best-seller. Cynthia is also a two-time finalist for the RITA® award (she was a finalist both in the romantic suspense category and in the paranormal romance category). Since she began writing full-time in 2005, Cynthia has written over thirty novels and novellas.

Cynthia is a southern girl who loves horror movies, chocolate, and happy endings. More information about Cynthia and her books may be found at: http://www.cynthiaeden.com or on her Facebook page at: http://www.facebook.com/cynthiaedenfanpage. Cynthia is also on Twitter at http://www.twitter.com/cynthiaeden.

Made in the USA
San Bernardino, CA
21 May 2018